THE HAUNTING OF
BLACKWOOD MANOR

The Haunting of Blackwood Manor

Doug Hensley

CONTENTS

1 – 1 1

1

The Haunting of Blackwood Mansion
by
Doug Hensley

Author's Notes

THE HAUNTING OF BLACKWOOD MANSION
THE DAVIS FAMILY THOUGHT THEIR LONG-LOST UNCLE HAD GIVEN THEM A FRESH START WHEN THEY INHERITED HIS SPRAWLING OLD MANSION HIDDEN DEEP IN THE WOODS. IF ANYONE HAD TAKEN THE TIME TO NOTICE WHAT WENT ON AROUND TOWN, HE HAD BEEN DARKLY INFAMOUS LOCALLY, SO MANSION LIFE QUICKLY REVEALS ITS VIOLENT UNDERBELLY IN MORE WAYS THAN ONE. PECULIAR THINGS BEGIN TO HAPPEN TO THE FAMILY FROM THE MOMENT THEY STEP THROUGH THE GRAND FRONT DOOR. UNSEEN FORCES TORMENT THEM, AND EERIE WHISPERS FILL THE NIGHT. THE TERROR ESCALATES WHEN MARY FINDS AN OLD CHEST IN THE ATTIC FILLED WITH BOOKS ABOUT WITCHCRAFT AND OUIJA BOARDS,

CULMINATING IN A TERRIBLE ENCOUNTER WITH A GHOSTLY WITCH HANGING FROM A TREE.

AS THE HAUNTING INTENSIFIES, EACH FAMILY MEMBER IS SUBJECTED TO A PLETHORA OF CHILLING VISIONS AND ENCOUNTERS WITH MALEVOLENT ENTITIES. THE SHADOWS DANCE OF THEIR OWN ACCORD, AND THERE IS A MENACING POLTERGEIST ON THE LOOSE. THEIR ONLY HOPE FOR SURVIVAL RESTS IN UNCOVERING THE DARK SECRETS OF THE MANSION AND FACING WHATEVER EVIL DWELLS WITHIN ITS CONFINES.

THE DAVIS FAMILY ENTERS THE MANSION, ASSISTED BY A MEDIUM AND AN HISTORIAN, TO SHOW ITS HORRIFIC HISTORY OF INVOLVEMENT WITH WITCHCRAFT AND SACRILEGIOUS RIGHTS. WITH THE HOUSE FACING THEM IN AN EVER-SQUEEZING VICE OF TERROR AND FEAR, THE FAMILY IS GOING TO ENDURE AN INCREDIBLE RITUAL PROCESS, RIFE WITH MOMENTS OF CONFRONTING DEEP PERSONAL FEARS.

A HAUNTING TALE OF COURAGE AND SURVIVAL, THE HAUNTING OF BLACKWOOD MANSION UNRAVELS INTO A STORY INVOLVING THE POWER OF FAMILY, WEIGHING HISTORY, AND AN ETERNAL BATTLE AGAINST DARKNESS. WILL THE SPIRITS OF THE DEAD OVERCOME THE PAST, OR WILL THESE BE THE NEW VICTIMS OF A MANSION'S CURSPREPARE TO TAKE A SPINE-TINGLING TOUR INTO A REALM WHERE THE SHADOWY OUTLINES TAKE LIFE AND NIGHTMARISH HISTORICAL EVENTS REFUSE TO BE BURIED.

TABLE OF CONTENTS

CHAPTER 1: THE INHERITANCE

THE FAMILY IS CONTACTED BY LETTER WITH NEWS THAT THEY HAVE BEEN BEQUEATHED AN OLD MANSION WHICH BELONGED TO JOHN'S ESTRANGED UNCLE.

THEY DECIDE TO MOVE IN, FEELING MYSTERIOUS AND CURIOUS ABOUT ITS VALUATION.

CHAPTER 2: FIRST IMPRESSIONS

THE FAMILY FINALLY ARRIVES AT THE MANSION AND IS IMPRESSED BY ITS GRANDEUR, THOUGH IT FEELS EERILY OUT OF PLACE.

STRANGE THINGS START TO HAPPEN: LIGHTS FLICKER, COLD SPOTS, AND WHISPERS MAY BE HEARD FROM AFAR.

CHAPTER 3: THE WICKED UNCLE'S LEGACY

MORE ABOUT THE UNCLE'S DARK NAME IS REVEALED THROUGH THE LOCALS SPEAKING OF WITCHCRAFT AND SINISTER RITUALS.

JOHN PUTS IT OFF AS SUPERSTITION, BUT MARY FEELS A LITTLE UNEASY.

CHAPTER 4: THE FIRST NIGHT

LUCY HAS A TERRIBLE NIGHTMARE OF BEING PURSUED THROUGH THE MANSION BY A SHADOWY FIGURE.

TOM HEARS FOOTSTEPS OUTSIDE HIS ROOM BUT FINDS NOBODY THERE.

CHAPTER 5: THE ATTIC DISCOVERY

MARY HEADS INTO THE ATTIC AND FINDS AN OLD BOX FULL OF OUIJA BOARDS, BOOKS ON WITCHCRAFT, AND SPELLS OF MAGIC. THEN, THROUGH THE ATTIC WINDOW, SHE SEES A VIEW OF A WITCH HUNG FROM A TREE, BUT EVERY TIME SHE RUNS DOWNSTAIRS OUTSIDE, THERE SHE FINDS NOTHING IN SIGHT.

CHAPTER 6: THE HAUNTING BEGINS
JOHN SEES HIS UNCLE'S GHOSTLY APPARITION IN THE STUDY HIMSELF, WARNING HIM TO LEAVE THE HOUSE.
MARY STARTS TO HEAR A WOMAN'S VOICE WHISPERING INCANTATIONS INTO HER EAR.

CHAPTER 7: LUCY'S POSSESSION
LUCY STARTS ACTING WEIRDLY: SHE SPEAKS SOME LANGUAGE NOBODY UNDERSTANDS AND DRAWS WEIRD SIGNS.
HER FAMILY BECOMES INCREASINGLY CONCERNED ABOUT HER BEHAVIOR.

CHAPTER 8: TOM'S ENCOUNTER
TOM IS CALLED DOWN TO THE BASEMENT BY THE VOICE OF A CHILD AND GETS LOCKED IN WITH SOME INVISIBLE ENTITY.
HE IS FOUND HOURS LATER IN SHOCK, REFUSING TO SPEAK OF WHAT HE HAS SEEN.

CHAPTER 9: THE WITCH'S CURSE
MARY GOES THROUGH THE BOOKS FROM THE ATTIC AND FINDS THE CURSE PLACED UPON THE MANSION BY A POWERFUL WITCH.
THE WITCH PROMISED VENGEANCE AGAINST ANY RELATION OF THE UNCLE.

CHAPTER 10: THE OUIJA BOARD
DESPERATE FOR ANSWERS, THE FAMILY USES ONE OF THE OUIJA BOARDS TO COMMUNICATE WITH THE SPIRITS.
THEY REACH A FRIENDLY SPIRIT WHO WARNS THEM ABOUT THE RETURN OF THE WITCH.

CHAPTER 11: THE POLTERGEIST
THE POLTERGEIST ACTIVITY INCREASES: THROWING OF OBJECTS, MOVEMENT OF FURNITURE, AND SLAPPING OF DOORS.
THE FAMILY WANTS TO GET OUT BUT IS HINDERED, SO TO

SAY, BY SOME UNSEEN FORCE.

CHAPTER 12: THE RETURN OF THE WITCH

THE SPIRIT OF THE WITCH MANIFESTS HERSELF MORE FREQUENTLY, APPEARING TO EACH MEMBER OF THE FAMILY AND TEASING THEM.

THEY REALIZE THEY MUST FIND A WAY TO BREAK THE CURSE TO SURVIVE.

CHAPTER 13: THE HIDDEN ROOM

TOM DISCOVERS A HIDDEN ROOM IN THE MANSION WITH MORE OF THE UNCLE'S DARK ARTIFACTS AND A JOURNAL. THE JOURNAL CONTAINS THE UNCLE'S PACT WITH THE WITCH AND HOW TO BREAK THE CURSE.

CHAPTER 14: THE RITUAL PREPARATION THE FAMILY PREPARES WHAT THEY NEED FOR A COUNTER-RITUAL TO BANISH THE WITCH'S SPIRIT. TENSIONS RISE AS THEY PREPARE FOR THE DANGEROUS TASK AHEAD.

CHAPTER 15: THE WITCH'S ATTACKON THE NIGHT OF THE RITUAL, THE SPIRIT OF THE WITCH GETS MORE AGGRESSIVE AND PHYSICALLY ATTACKS THE FAMILY.

THEY TRY TO DEFEND AGAINST THE ATTACKS WHILE CONTINUING THE RITUAL.

CHAPTER 16: THE FINAL CONFRONTATION

THE FAMILY STARTS THE RITUAL, RECITING INCANTATIONS AND USING THE ARTIFACTS.

THE WITCH'S SPIRIT FIGHTS BACK FIERCELY, ALMOST OVERPOWERING THEM.

CHAPTER 17: THE SACRIFICE

MARY REALIZES A PERSONAL SACRIFICE IS NEEDED TO COMPLETE THE RITUAL.

SHE OFFERS HERSELF, AND THE WITCH'S SPIRIT CLINGS TO HER; THE OTHERS MANAGE TO FINISH THE RITUAL.

CHAPTER 18: THE BREAKING OF THE CURSE

THE FINAL INCANTATION FREES THE WITCH'S SPIRIT AND

REMOVES THE CURSE.
THE MANSION RELAPSES INTO CREEPY SILENCE.

CHAPTER 19: AFTER

THE FAMILY TAKES TIME TO CONTEMPLATE THEIR HARROWING EXPERIENCE AND THE LOSS THEY FACED. THEY GLADLY LEAVE THE MANSION BEHIND THEM, THANKFUL FOR JUST BEING ALIVE.

CHAPTER 20 A NEW BEGINNING

THE FAMILY MOVES TO A NEW HOUSE, FAR AWAY FROM THE MANSION AND ITS DARK INHERITANCE.
THEY GET PEACE, BUT THERE ARE HINTS OF THE FACT THAT THE WITCH'S INFLUENCE IS NOT FULLY GONE YET.

****

CHAPTER 1 THE INHERITANCE

THE MORNING WAS OVERCAST, AND THERE WAS A SOMBER GRAY LIGHT THAT TENDED TO PERMEATE THE LITTLE SUBURBAN HOME BELONGING TO THE DAVIS FAMILY. JOHN DAVIS SAT AT THE BREAKFAST TABLE, SIPPING HIS COFFEE AND READING THE NEWSPAPER. HIS WIFE MARY WAS AN GENTLE WOMAN WITH AN ENQUIRING MIND, BUSYING HERSELF WITH PREPARING BREAKFAST FOR THEIR TWO CHILDREN, LUCY AND TOM.

JUST AS LUCY, A PRECOCIOUS, IMAGINATIVE TEENAGER, WAS BOUNCING DOWN THE STAIRS, THE DOORBELL RANG. BEHIND HER WAS TOM, A QUIET, INTROSPECTIVE BOY, RUBBING THE SLEEP FROM HIS EYES. JOHN GOT UP TO ANSWER THE DOOR AND FOUND A SERIOUS-LOOKING MAN IN A DARK SUIT HOLDING A LETTER AT IT.

"MR. DAVIS?" HE ASKED.

"YES, THAT'S ME," JOHN ANSWERED, PUZZLED.

THE MAN HANDED HIM THE LETTER. "I AM THE EXECUTOR OF YOUR LATE UNCLE, BARTHOLOMEW DAVIS'S ESTATE.

THIS IS FOR YOU."

JOHN TOOK THE LETTER, HIS MIND RACING. HE COULD HARDLY REMEMBER HIS UNCLE BARTHOLOMEW, A RECLUSE AND AN ECCENTRIC WHO HAD SEVERED ALL LINKS WITH THE FAMILY MANY YEARS AGO. HE WATCHED AS THE MAN WALKED AWAY BEFORE CLOSING THE DOOR AND RETURNING TO THE KITCHEN.

"WHO WAS THAT?" MARY ASKED, PLACING A PLATE OF PANCAKES ON THE TABLE.

JOHN HELD UP THE LETTER. "A LAWYER. APPARENTLY, MY UNCLE BARTHOLOMEW DIED AND LEFT US SOMETHING IN HIS WILL."

LUCY AND TOM LOOKED AT EACH OTHER CURIOUSLY AS JOHN OPENED THE ENVELOPE. INSIDE WAS A LETTER ON AGED, YELLOWED PAPER WITH AN ELABORATE HANDWRITING.

"DEAR JOHN," HE READ ALOUD, "I HOPE THIS LETTER FINDS YOU IN GOOD HEALTH. I AM WRITING TO YOU WITH A VERY HEAVY HEART TO INFORM YOU OF THE PASSING OF YOUR UNCLE BARTHOLOMEW. BEING HIS ONLY SURVIVING RELATIVE, HE HAS WILLED HIS ESTATE TO YOU, INCLUSIVE OF THE MANSION IN THE WOODS. IT IS NOW MY DUTY TO MAKE YOU AWARE OF THIS FACT AND TO ASSIST YOU IN ANY POSSIBLE WAY. SINCERELY, ARTHUR GRAHAM, ESQ."

MARY'S EYES WENT WIDE. "A MANSION? OUT IN THE WOODS? IT SOUNDS LIKE SOMETHING FROM A GOTHIC NOVEL."

JOHN SPOKE THOUGHTFULLY. "I CAN BARELY REMEMBER BARTHOLOMEW—HE WAS ALWAYS A BIT. ODD. STILL, A MANSION COULD BE VERY VALUABLE."

LUCY WAS ALREADY LEANING FORWARD, EAGERLY. "CAN WE GO SEE IT, DAD? THAT WOULD BE SO COOL!"

TOM, EVER CAUTIOUS, FROWNED. "WHAT IF IT'S HAUNTED

OR SOMETHING?

JOHN CHUCKLED. "I DOUBT THAT, TOM, BUT WE REALLY OUGHT TO CHECK IT OUT. PERHAPS IT'S TIME FOR A LITTLE ADVENTURE."

A WEEK LATER, THE DAVIS FAMILY PACKED THEIR BELONGINGS INTO THEIR CAR AND SET OFF FOR THE MANSION. THE JOURNEY TOOK THEM ALONG WINDING COUNTRY ROADS, THROUGH FIELDS AND FORESTS, AS THE LANDSCAPE GREW MORE REMOTE AND WILD.

THE SKY GREW DARKER AS THEY APPROACHED THE EDGE OF THE WOODS. MARY GLANCED AT THE MAP, FROWNING. "ARE YOU SURE THIS IS THE RIGHT WAY, JOHN? IT FEELS LIKE WE'RE IN THE MIDDLE OF NOWHERE."

JOHN NODDED. "THE DIRECTIONS SAY IT'S JUST UP AHEAD. LOOK, THERE'S A SIGN."

SURE ENOUGH, AN OLD, WEATHERED SIGN POINTED DOWN A NARROW, OVERGROWN PATH. IT READ: "DAVIS MANOR."

AS THEY MADE THE TURN ONTO THE PATH, THE TREES BEGAN TO CLOSE IN, THEIR BRANCHES ARCING OVER THE CAR AND SHUTTING OUT THE SKY. IT GREW COOLER AND AN APPREHENSIVE FEELING SETTLED OVER THE FAMILY.

"ARE WE THERE YET?" LUCY ASKED, PEERING OUT THE WINDOW.

"ALMOST," JOHN REPLIED, CLUTCHING AT THE WHEEL.

FINALLY, THEY EMERGED FROM THE TUNNEL OF TREES INTO A CLEARING. STANDING BEFORE THEM, AN IMPOSING MANSION THREE STORIES TALL ROSE HIGH WITH A ONCE PROUD FACADE NOW IN RUIN, ENGULFED IN A HEAVY GROWTH OF IVY. THE WINDOWS WERE BLACK AND EMPTY, EYES OF A LONG-FORGOTTEN GHOST.

"WOAH," MARY BREATHED. "IT'S. MAGNIFICENT. AND CREEPY."

THEY PARKED THE CAR AND STEPPED OUT, GAZING UP IN

awe and apprehension at the mansion. A gentle breeze swept through the trees, causing them to rustle, and it seemed as though the old house groaned in response.

John took a deep breath. "Well, let's go inside."

The front door creaked ominously as John shoved it open onto a grand foyer with a sweeping staircase and high, vaulted ceilings. Pale light filtered in grimy windowpanes dancing motes of dust. "It's so cold in here," Mary said, shivering. Lucy and Tom continued to walk further, wandering through the deserted rooms and echoing down empty halls, while Mary and John walked, the latter doing so a great deal more hesitantly and gazing in wonder at faded opulence, at chandeliers hanging down from the ceilings with crystals now dulled by dust and old portraits framing the walls of people staring from them with empty eyes.

"This place must have been beautiful once," Mary said, running her fingers over a cracked banister.

John nodded. "It's still impressive. But it'll need a lot of work."

Suddenly, Lucy's voice echoed down the hall. "Mom, Dad, come look at this!"

They hurried to find her standing in a large, ornate parlor. A massive fireplace dominated one wall and a grand piano sat in the corner, its keys yellowed with age.

"Isn't it amazing?" Lucy said, her eyes shining with excitement.

Tom, who had been quiet up to this time, suddenly spoke up. "You think Uncle Bartholomew really

LIVED HERE ALL BY HIMSELF?"

JOHN SHRUGGED. "HE WAS KIND OF A RECLUSE. BUT NOW IT'S OURS."

AND AS THEY EXPLORED FURTHER, THEY FOUND MORE SIGNS OF THE MANSION'S FORMER GLORY: A LIBRARY FILLED WITH DUSTY BOOKS, A DINING ROOM WITH A LONG, POLISHED TABLE, AND A BALLROOM WITH A CHANDELIER THAT SPARKLED FAINTLY IN THE DIM LIGHT.

YET THERE WERE ALSO SIGNS OF NEGLECT AND ROT. THE WALLPAPER WAS TORN, THE FLOORBOARDS CREAKED, AND STRANGE MUSTY ODORS HAD SEEPED INTO THE AIR.

LATER THAT EVENING, THEY GATHERED IN THE KITCHEN TO PREPARE A SIMPLE MEAL THEY HAD PACKED WITH THEM. ABOVE THE SILENT DINNER, THE ATMOSPHERE SWIRLED, HEAVY WITH AN OMINOUS SILENCE-ONLY THE ODD CREAK OR FAR-OFF RUSTLING OF LEAVES BROKE IT.

"DO YOU THINK WE'LL GET TO SEE ANY GHOSTS?" LUCY ASKED HALF-SERIOUS.

JOHN CHUCKLED. "I DOUBT IT. BUT WE'LL BE NEEDING TO GET SOME PROPER LIGHTS IN HERE. IT'S TOO DARK."

MARY LOOKED OUT OF THE WINDOW AT THE ONCOMING WOODS. "WE ALSO NEED TO INVESTIGATE THE GROUNDS. MAKE SURE EVERYTHING'S OKAY."

AS THEY SETTLED IN FOR THE NIGHT, THAT SENSE OF UNEASE LINGERED. THE MANSION WAS FULL OF SECRETS, AND THEY COULD FEEL THEM PRESSING IN FROM THE SHADOWS.

UPSTAIRS, THE FAMILY RETIRED TO SEPARATE BEDROOMS, EACH CONTAINING AN ANTIQUE BED AND HEAVY DRAPES THAT LET LITTLE WARMTH IN AND KEPT OUT THE CHILL. MARY AND JOHN LAY IN THEIR BED; THE SILENCE OF THE MANSION PRESSED IN AROUND THEM.

"DO YOU THINK THIS WAS A GOOD IDEA?" MARY

WHISPERED, BARELY AUDIBLE.

JOHN SIGHED. "I DON'T KNOW. BUT WE HAVE TO AT LEAST TRY. THIS PLACE COULD BE WORTH A FORTUNE IF WE FIX IT UP."

MARY NODDED, HER UNEASE REFUSING TO DISSIPATE. SHE ROLLED OVER AND SHUT HER EYES, TRYING TO SLEEP.

IN THE ROOM NEXT DOOR, LUCY LAY AWAKE STARING AT THE CEILING. SHE HEARD THE FAINTEST SOUNDS OF THE HOUSE SETTLING—THE CREAKS AND GROANS THAT SEEMED TO BE ALMOST A WHISPER. SHE SHIVERED AND PULLED THE COVERS UP UNDER HER CHIN.

TOM, UPSTAIRS, WAS LYING IN THE DARK, LISTENING. HE FELT SOMEBODY PASS ALONG THE HALL, BUT WHEN HE OPENED THE DOOR NO ONE WAS THERE.

BY NIGHT THE FAMILY LAY IN A SORT OF STUPOR, NOT HAVING RECOVERED FROM THE EVENTS OF THE DAY, WHILE THE EYES OUT THERE IN THE DARK WATCHED EVERY MOVE THAT WAS MADE.

IN THE MIDDLE OF THE NIGHT, LUCY WOKE WITH A START, HER HEART RACING WILDLY. SHE HAD BEEN DREAMING THAT SOME FORM WAS CHASING HER DOWN THE HALLS OF THIS MANSION, ITS FACE HIDDEN IN SHADOW. SHE SAT UP, TRYING TO SHAKE OFF THE LINGERING FEAR.

SHE TURNED TO HER BEDSIDE TABLE AND GLANCED AT THE CLOCK. IT WAS JUST A LITTLE AFTER MIDNIGHT. SHE TOOK A DEEP BREATH AND LAY BACK, BUT SLEEP WAS ELUSIVE.

NEXT DOOR, MARY ALSO LAY AWAKE, HAUNTED BY A DREAM OF SOME WOMAN'S VOICE WHISPERING INTO HER EAR. SHE SAT UP AND TURNED TO THE DARKENED ROOM, GROWING INCREASINGLY UNEASY.

JOHN SLEPT FITFULLY BESIDE HER, UNAWARE OF THE STRANGE PRESENCE THAT SEEMED TO FILL THE ROOM.

In the early hours of the morning, Tom woke to the sound of a door creaking open. He sat up, his heart racing, and listened. The sound came again, followed by the faintest whisper of footsteps.

He got out of bed and crept to his door, peering out into the hallway. It was empty, but the air felt heavy and oppressive.

He closed his door and climbed back into bed, pulling the covers over his head. It was a long time before he fell back asleep.

The next morning, the family gathered in the kitchen, each of them looking tired and on edge.

"Anyone else have weird dreams last night?" Lucy asked, eyes wide.

Mary nodded. "I did. I kept hearing some woman's voice."

John frowned. "I didn't dream, but it was like something watched us."

Tom just looked down at his plate, silent and pale.

"We should probably start cleaning up and getting this place in order," John said, trying to sound chipper. "The sooner we make it our own, the better."

They'd spent the day cleaning and exploring, trying to push off the unease that had settled over them. But the mansion seemed to fight them at every turn, its shadows growing darker and more oppressive as the day wore on.

Later that afternoon, Mary went up to the attic, looking for old furniture they could use. She climbed the narrow stairs up, her feet echoing in the silence.

The attic was dark and dusty, cluttered with

TRUNKS AND OTHER FURNITURE COVERED WITH COBWEBS. MARY COUGHED AS SHE SQUEEZED HER WAY THROUGH THE CLUTTERED SPACE, THE FLASHLIGHT IN HER HAND FLICKERING.

SHE NOTICED AN OLD CHEST STANDING IN ONE CORNER; THE COLOR OF THE WOOD WAS WORN OUT AND WEATHERED. CURIOUS, SHE OPENED IT AND GASPED. INSIDE WERE OUIJA BOARDS, WITCHCRAFT BOOKS, AND SPELLS, THE PAGES YELLOW WITH AGE.

AS SHE STARED AT THE CONTENTS OF THE CHEST, A CHILL RAN DOWN HER SPINE. SHE FELT LIKE SOMEONE WAS WATCHING HER. SHE TURNED SLOWLY AND SAW, THROUGH THE GRIMY ATTIC WINDOW, A FIGURE HANGING FROM A TREE.

IT WAS A WOMAN, HER FACE TWISTED IN A GRIMACE OF PAIN, HER EYES STARING BLANKLY. MARY SCREAMED AND STUMBLED BACK, HER HEART RACING.

SHE WAS DOWNSTAIRS IN AN INSTANT, FLINGING OPEN THE DOOR AS SHE CALLED HIS NAME. DOWN TO THE TREE AND-NOTHING. NO ONE.

JOHN LOOKED AT HER QUESTIONINGLY. "ARE YOU CERTAIN YOU SAW SOMEBODY?"

MARY NODDED HER HEAD, STILL TREMBLING. "I KNOW I SAW HER, JOHN."

THEY WERE IN A STAND OF WOODS IN THE CIRCLE DRIVE, TREES QUIET SAVE FOR SOFT, GENTLE, INSISTENT MURMURS THROUGH THE LEAVES, WITH THE MANSION BROODING BEHIND.

THE SENSE OF FOREBODING HAD DEEPENED AS THEY WENT BACK INSIDE. SECRETS FILLED THE MANSION, AND these were only just beginning to unravel before the Davis family.

Chapter 2: First Impressions

Part 1: The Mansion's Embrace

The day dawned with a mist clinging to the ground, wrappings of an ethereal, almost otherworldly shroud, about the mansion. The Davis family, still recovering from the unsettling night before, gathered in the kitchen for breakfast. The old stove of the mansion creaked and groaned its way through heating their food, adding to the atmosphere of decay.

"Anyone else hear that noise last night?" Lucy finally spoke up, shattering the silence. Her eyes were wide with a mix of excitement and fear.

Mary nodded palely. "It wasn't just noise. I saw something. Someone in the attic window."

John tried to make the day as normal as possible. He forced a smile. "Old houses make strange noises. Let's not get ahead of ourselves."

Tom was subdued and introspective, playing with the food on his plate. He hadn't said anything about the footsteps in the hall, the whispering that seemed to issue from nowhere.

They set out, after breakfast, to take a more thorough view of the mansion. The magnificent staircase was dusty, an amazing feat in the use of beauty, with its complicated banisters and shining wood. The stairs groaned under their footsteps as they ascended; the echo sounded through the great empty halls.

The second floor was a maze of rooms, each one more interesting and unsettling than the last.

There was a library of ancient books, their leather covers cracked, their pages yellow. Lucy was delighted, but Mary felt a shiver run down her spine as she picked up a book dealing with occult practices.

"These must have belonged to Bartholomew," John said, scanning the titles. "He always had a taste for the unusual."

Tom stepped into what might once have served as a study: a very large oak desk stood there with lots of old papers lying all over, old quills besides them. One book lay opened on the desk, and to this book, Tom felt some weird attraction. He went nearer, the cold was instantly greater; the whispering of strange words he knew sounded in his ears now. He beat a hasty retreat, his heart racing.

Meanwhile, Lucy had found her way to a bedroom with heavy drapes and an ornate canopy bed. As she explored, suddenly there was a chill, and she turned to see the shadowy trace of a form dance upon the wall. She gasped and ran out into the hall, her footsteps echoing off the empty hallways.

The family reunited in the middle of the afternoon in the parlor, a growing sense of unease building in each of them. The once-grand room, with its decaying grandeur, seemed to close in around them.

"We should stay together," John said. "It's a big place, and it's easy to get lost."

They decided to get some fresh air, hoping that it would break some of the tension. The backyard was an overgrown garden, sprawling out with winding paths through tangled underbrush and hidden clearings. An old, dry fountain sat cracked in the middle, surrounded by stone benches.

As they strolled along, Lucy stopped dead in her tracks. "Do you hear that?" she whispered.

The rest hushed and, indeed, could hear it-a faint, almost melodious humming that seemed to be coming from everywhere and nowhere all at once.

"Probably just the wind," John said-but he didn't sound convinced.

They followed the sound, which led them to a small, ramshackle greenhouse. The glass was cracked and smeared with grime, and the door hung ajar. Inside, they found a collection of dead plants and broken pots. The humming grew louder, more distinct, and as they stepped further inside, the air grew thick and heavy.

Mary came to a very large pot, and as she looked into it, a swarm of insects burst forth, buzzing angrily. She screamed and fell back, her heart racing.

"We need to be careful," John said, his voice steady but tight. "This place is old and falling apart."

As they went out of the greenhouse, Lucy remained behind and walked towards some trees that lined up along the perimeter of the lot. This was an uncanny pull; it felt like the trees were beckoning her. Gradually, she moved toward one lone big oak amidst the grove.

Suddenly, a hand was laid on her shoulder. She spun around, expecting to see one of her family members, but there was no one there. The air grew colder, and she could hear the faint sound of laughter-high and cruel. She ran back to her family, her heart pounding in her chest.

The darkness started falling, and the family finally headed back into the mansion; heavy was the feeling in the air. They gathered in the parlor and lit candles as the darkness gradually surrounded them. The dancing flame licked across the walls and threw long shadows-a weird, twisting tableaux.

"I think we should research this place," Mary said. "There's bound to be some record or something to tell us just what's happening."

John nodded in agreement. "I'll go into town tomorrow and see what I can find at the library."

As night wore on, it grew colder and the wind howled outside, the windows rattling ominously. The family sat huddled together, trying to shut out the sounds that seemed to come from the very walls around them.

Lucy couldn't get rid of the feeling that she was being watched. Every creak and groan of the house set her nerves on edge. She glanced at the portraits on the walls, their eyes seeming to follow her every move.

Tom was on edge, too-he kept thinking he heard whispers, soundless and just within earshot, as if someone were speaking right inside his mind. He tried to focus on his family, but the voices grew louder, more insistent.

Mary got up to make tea, hoping it would soothe her jangling nerves. She was halfway to the kitchen when a cold draft seemed to whisk past

HER. SHE WHIRLED, BUT THERE WAS NO ONE IN SIGHT. SHADOWS DANCED AND WRITHED IN THE CANDLELIGHT, FORMING SHAPES THAT DISAPPEARED WHEN SHE TURNED TO CONFRONT THEM.

IN THE KITCHEN, SHE FOUND AN OLD KETTLE AND FILLED IT WITH WATER. WHILE WAITING FOR ITS BOILING, SHE HAPPENED TO NOTICE A DOOR THAT HAD ESCAPED HER ATTENTION. THE DOOR, A LITTLE AJAR, CREAKED OPEN DOWN TO SEEMINGLY A CELLAR. CURIOSITY SNUFFED OUT THE THREAD OF FEAR AS SHE SLOWLY OPENED THE DOOR FURTHER AND PEERED INTO THE DARKNESS.

THE STEPS CREAKED AS SHE WENT DOWN, THE AIR GROWING COLDER WITH EACH STEP. SHE REACHED THE BOTTOM AND FOUND HERSELF IN A SMALL, DIMLY LIT ROOM. SHELVES LINED THE WALLS, FILLED WITH JARS OF STRANGE, PRESERVED SPECIMENS. AN OLD WORKBENCH STOOD IN THE CENTER, COVERED IN DUSTY TOOLS AND MYSTERIOUS VIALS.

MARY SHIVERED, FEELING AS IF THE WALLS WERE CLOSING IN ON HER. SHE TURNED TO LEAVE, BUT SOMETHING CAUGHT HER EYE—A SMALL, LEATHER-BOUND BOOK ON THE WORKBENCH. SHE PICKED IT UP AND FLIPPED THROUGH THE PAGES, HER HEART RACING AS SHE READ THE STRANGE SYMBOLS AND INCANTATIONS.

IT SWUNG SHUT SUDDENLY, PLUNGING THE ROOM INTO DARKNESS. MARY SHRIEKED AND FUMBLED FOR HER FLASHLIGHT WITH TREMBLING HANDS. SHE CLICKED IT ON AND, IN THE DOORFRAME, SHE SAW A FIGURE DRAPED IN DARKNESS.

THE SCREAM FROM MARY WAS HEARD THROUGHOUT THE MANSION AS JOHN, LUCY, AND TOM CAME RUNNING. THEY FOUND HER PALE AND QUIVERING IN THE KITCHEN, CLUTCHING THE LITTLE BOOK.

"WHAT'S WRONG?" JOHN ASKED, HIS EYES WIDE WITH WORRY.

MARY NODDED TOWARD THE DOOR INTO THE CELLAR. "I FOUND THIS BOOK DOWN THERE. AND. AND I SAW SOMETHING."

JOHN TOOK THE BOOK AND GLANCED AT IT, FROWNING. "WE NEED TO BE CAREFUL. THIS PLACE IS. UNSETTLING, TO SAY THE LEAST."

THEY DECIDED TO LEAVE THE CELLAR FOR THE TIME BEING, FEELING THAT THEY HAD ALREADY PUSHED THEIR LUCK. THEY WENT BACK INTO THE PARLOR, THE SENSE OF UNEASE GROWING WITH EVERY SECOND.

AS NIGHT WORE ON, THE MANSION SEEMED TO COME ALIVE. THE SOUND OF FOOTSTEPS ECHOED THROUGH THE HALLS, DOORS CREAKED OPEN AND SHUT, AND THE WHISPERING GREW LOUDER, MORE INSISTENT.

SLEEPLESS, LUCY DRIFTED DOWN THE DARKENED HALLWAY, BEGUILED BY A FAINT THREAD OF MUSIC UNTIL IT LED HER INTO THE LIBRARY, WHERE AN ANTIQUE GRAMOPHONE PLAYED A MELODY SAD AND HAUNTING. THE ROOM WAS DESERTED, YET A PRESENCE SEEMED TO STARE AT HER.

TOM WAS RESTLESS TOO, SAT IN HIS ROOM STARING AT THE WALLS AS THE WHISPERS MOUNTED IN HIS HEAD, UNTIL A COMPULSION HE HAD NEVER FELT TOOK HIM TO THE ATTIC WHERE MARY SAW THE FIGURE HANGING.

HE SLOWLY CLIMBED UP THE STAIRS TO THE ATTIC WITH HIS HEART IN HIS MOUTH, COLD AND FILLED WITH THICK DUSTY AIR. THIS IS WHERE ALL THAT MALEVOLENCE WATCHED ME FROM, FEELING THE PRESENCE. HE TURNED TOWARDS THE DOOR; THE DOOR WAS SHUT BEHIND HIS BACK. NOW, HE GOT TRAPPED INTO THE DARKNESS OF THE ATTIC ROOM.

JOHN AND MARY SAT IN THE PARLOR TRYING TO MAKE SENSE OF IT ALL. JOHN FLIPPED THROUGH THE BOOK THAT MARY HAD FOUND; HIS FACE GREW MORE SERIOUS WITH EACH PAGE. "THIS IS SOME SORT OF SPELLBOOK," HE SAID. "IT EXPLAINS MUCH ABOUT BARTHOLOMEW'S INTERESTS. IT ALSO MENTIONS A CURSE OF SOME SORT."

MARY SHIVERED. "WE MUST FIND A WAY TO LIFT IT. WE CANNOT REMAIN HERE LIKE THIS."

THE CRASHING SOUND UPSTAIRS CAME LOUD, MAKING THEM RUSH TOWARD FINDING LUCY AND TOM. AT THIS MOMENT, THEIR FEAR BECAME GREATER. IN THE LIBRARY, THEY FOUND LUCY, WHO LOOKED AT THE GRAMOPHONE IN SHOCK.

"IT JUST STARTED TO PLAY ON ITS OWN," SHE WHISPERED. THEY RUSHED UPSTAIRS TO THE ATTIC; HE WAS PALE AND TREMBLING, WITH THE DOOR CLOSED FAST. JOHN FORCED IT OPEN, AND OUT TUMBLED TOM, HIS EYES WIDE WITH TERROR.

"WE NEED TO LEAVE," HE SAID IN A SHAKING VOICE. "THERE'S SOMETHING EVIL HERE."

JOHN NODDED, HIS EXPRESSION GRIM. "WE'LL LEAVE TOMORROW. BUT FOR NOW, LET'S STAY TOGETHER."

THEY PASSED THE REMAINDER OF THE NIGHT IN THE PARLOR, HUDDLED TOGETHER, AS IF THE SHADOWS SEEMED TO PRESS AROUND THEM, AND THE MANSION WHISPERED DARK SECRETS INTO THEIR EARS. THE DAVIS FAMILY CAME FOR AN INHERITANCE BUT FOUND SO MUCH MORE-SINISTER-AND ONE THAT WOULD NOT LET THEM GO SO EASILY.

CHAPTER 3: THE FIRST NIGHT'S GRIP

The dawn's light did little to dispel the darkness that had settled over the Davis family. The mansion, once a distant and eerie curiosity, now felt like a malevolent entity, wrapping them in a suffocating embrace. The family gathered in the parlor, their faces drawn and pale from a sleepless night filled with unnerving noises and unsettling dreams.

Mary looked at John, her eyes reflecting the fear and uncertainty that had taken root. "We need to get out of here, John. We can't stay another night in this house."

John nodded, his resolve weakening. "I agree. I'll head into town and see if I can find out more about this place and maybe arrange for us to stay somewhere else."

Lucy and Tom, still shaken from their experiences, stayed close to their mother as John prepared to leave. As he walked out the door, a sense of foreboding filled the air, as if the house itself knew he was trying to escape its grasp.

John drove into town, the winding roads through the forest amplifying his sense of isolation. The small town was quiet, almost eerily so, as he pulled into the parking lot of the local library. He hoped to find some records or historical documents that might shed light on his uncle's mansion and the strange occurrences within it.

Inside the library, John was greeted by an elderly librarian who eyed him with a mixture of curiosity and wariness. "Can I help you, sir?" she asked, her voice tinged with a hint of suspicion.

John explained his situation, and the librarian's expression softened. "Ah, the old Davis mansion," she said, shaking her head. "It's been abandoned for years. Your uncle Bartholomew was a strange man. There are many stories about that place, none of them good."

She led him to a section of the library filled with old newspapers and historical records. "You'll find what you're looking for here," she said, leaving him to his research.

John spent hours poring over the documents, uncovering a dark history filled with tales of witchcraft, mysterious disappearances, and a curse that plagued the Davis family for generations. The more he read, the more he felt a sense of dread settle over him.

Meanwhile, back at the mansion, Mary, Lucy, and Tom tried to keep themselves occupied, but the house seemed determined to keep them on edge. Every creak of the floorboards, every gust of wind rattling the windows, sent chills down their spines.

Mary decided to explore the attic again, hoping to find more clues about Bartholomew's activities. She climbed the narrow staircase, her heart pounding with each step. The attic was as she remembered it—dim, dusty, and filled with the relics of a past she didn't understand.

As she sifted through the old trunks and boxes, she found more books on witchcraft and the occult. One book, in particular, caught her eye. It was bound in leather, with strange symbols etched into its cover. As she opened it, a gust of cold air swept through the attic, and the pages began to turn on their own.

Mary's heart raced as she tried to make sense of the cryptic text. The book seemed to be a diary of sorts, filled with Bartholomew's notes on rituals and spells. She felt a chill run down her spine as she read about his attempts to summon spirits and harness dark powers.

Suddenly, she heard a faint whisper, like a voice carried on the wind. She turned, expecting to see someone behind her, but the attic was empty. The whispering grew louder, more insistent, and she realized it was coming from the book itself.

Panicking, she slammed the book shut and fled the attic, her mind racing with fear and confusion. She found Lucy and Tom in the parlor, their faces pale and worried.

"Mom, are you okay?" Lucy asked, her voice trembling.

Mary nodded, but her hands were still shaking. "We need to stay together. This house is dangerous."

As the day wore on, the atmosphere in the mansion grew increasingly oppressive. The family felt as though they were being watched, and every room seemed to hold a dark secret waiting to be uncovered.

John returned from the library with a stack of documents and a grim expression. He gathered the family in the parlor and shared what he had learned.

"The mansion has a long history of strange occurrences and tragic events," John said, his voice heavy with the weight of his findings. "Bartholomew was deeply involved in the occult, and it seems he was trying to summon something... something dark."

Mary's face grew pale. "I found more books in the attic, including a diary of sorts. Bartholomew was obsessed with these rituals."

Tom, his fear palpable, asked, "What do we do now, Dad?"

John sighed. "We need to find a way to lift this curse. There must be something in these documents that can help us."

As they sifted through the papers, the house seemed to grow restless. The air grew colder, and the whispering voices returned, filling their ears with unintelligible murmurs. The lights flickered, casting eerie shadows on the walls.

Suddenly, a loud crash echoed through the house, and the family jumped in fright. They rushed to the source of the noise, finding the library in disarray. Books had been thrown from the shelves, and the gramophone was playing a haunting melody on its own.

"This house is trying to scare us," Lucy said, her voice trembling. "It doesn't want us here."

John set his jaw in determination. "We're not going to let it win. Let's focus on finding a solution."

As they continued their research, strange things began to happen with increasing frequency. Doors slammed shut, objects moved on their own, and the whispering voices grew louder, more insistent. The family struggled to stay calm, but the constant barrage of supernatural activity wore on their nerves.

One evening, as they gathered for dinner, the temperature in the dining room suddenly plummeted. Their breath came out in frosty puffs, and a dense fog filled the room. The shadows on the walls seemed to move, taking on sinister shapes.

Tom, unable to contain his fear, shouted, "Leave us alone!" His voice echoed through the room, but the shadows only grew darker, more menacing.

Mary grabbed his hand, her voice steady despite her fear. "We need to stay strong. We can't let this house break us."

John, his face grim, stood and addressed the unseen presence. "We will find a way to lift this curse. We will free this house from whatever darkness holds it."

The fog began to dissipate, and the temperature slowly returned to normal. The shadows receded, but the sense of unease remained. The family knew they were in a battle for their very souls, and they couldn't afford to lose.

Determined to find answers, the family decided to revisit the attic, hoping to uncover more of Bartholomew's secrets. They climbed the narrow staircase, their footsteps echoing in the silence. The attic was as Mary had left it, filled with old trunks and boxes, the air heavy with dust and decay.

John and Mary searched through the trunks, finding more books and strange artifacts. Lucy and Tom explored the far corners of the attic, their flashlights casting long shadows on the walls.

As they searched, Lucy found an old portrait of a woman with piercing eyes and a stern expression. The plaque beneath the portrait read: "Isabella Davis, 1865." She called her parents over, and they examined the painting closely.

"Isabella was one of our ancestors," John said. "There's a mention of her in the documents I found. She was accused of witchcraft and executed."

Mary's eyes widened. "Maybe she has something to do with the curse."

They continued to search, and Tom found a hidden compartment in one of the trunks. Inside was a small, ornate box with intricate carvings. He opened it carefully, revealing a collection of old letters and a journal.

The letters were written by Bartholomew and addressed to someone named Alistair. They detailed his experiments with dark magic and his attempts to contact spirits. The journal, written in Bartholomew's meticulous handwriting, contained notes on rituals and incantations.

John read aloud from the journal, his voice steady. "Bartholomew believed that the spirits of our ancestors were trapped in this house, bound by a curse that could only be broken by a blood relative."

Mary's face grew pale. "We need to perform the ritual to free them."

As they prepared to leave the attic, they heard a faint whisper, like a voice carried on the wind. It grew louder, more distinct, and they realized it was coming from the portrait of Isabella.

"Help us," the voice pleaded. "Free us from this torment."

The family exchanged frightened glances but knew they couldn't ignore the plea. They returned to the parlor, the journal and letters in hand, and began to plan the ritual.

That night, as the moon rose high in the sky, the Davis family prepared for the ritual. The instructions in Bartholomew's journal were detailed and specific, outlining the steps they needed to take to break the curse.

They gathered in the parlor, the air heavy with anticipation. John lit candles and arranged them in a circle, while Mary set out the items they needed: a silver chalice, a piece of Isabella's portrait, and a lock of hair from each family member.

The atmosphere grew tense as they began the ritual. John recited the incantations from the journal, his voice steady and confident. Mary and the children joined hands, their eyes closed in concentration.

As John spoke the final words of the incantation, the candles flickered and the air grew colder. The shadows in the room seemed to come alive, swirling around them in a chaotic dance.

Suddenly, a powerful gust of wind swept through the room, extinguishing the candles and plunging them into darkness. The whispering voices grew louder, filling their ears with a cacophony of sound.

John shouted over the noise, "Hold on! We're almost there!"

The room seemed to tilt, and the family struggled to keep their balance. The shadows closed in, and they felt a suffocating pressure, as if the very walls were closing in on them.

Then, as abruptly as it began, the chaos stopped. The candles relit themselves, and the room returned to normal. The air was still, and the whispering voices were gone.

The family stood in stunned silence, their hearts racing. They felt a sense of peace settle over them, as if a great weight had been lifted.

"Did it work?" Lucy asked, her voice trembling.

John nodded, his face pale but relieved. "I think so. The curse is broken."

As they looked around the room, they saw the portraits on the walls had changed. Isabella's stern expression was now one of peace, and the other ancestors looked serene.

The family hugged each other, tears of relief streaming down their faces. They had faced the darkness and emerged victorious, freeing their ancestors and breaking the curse that had plagued their family for generations.

But as they prepared to leave the mansion, a final whisper echoed through the room, chilling them to the bone: "Thank you... but beware. The darkness is never truly gone."

The family left the mansion, their hearts heavy with the knowledge that they had freed their ancestors but aware that the battle against darkness was never truly over. They vowed to stay together, to protect each other, and to remember the lessons they had learned in the old, haunted mansion.

CHAPTER 4: THE HAUNTING INTENSIFIES

The Davis family left the mansion, seeking refuge in a small, cozy inn at the edge of town. Exhausted from their ordeal, they hoped for a night of peaceful sleep. However, the sense of relief they felt was short-lived.

Mary awoke in the middle of the night, drenched in sweat and shivering despite the warmth of the room. She had dreamt of the mansion—its dark halls and whispering shadows calling out to her. Unable to shake the feeling of being watched, she got out of bed and tiptoed to the window. The moon cast a pale glow over the town, but the silhouette of the mansion loomed ominously in the distance.

John stirred and sat up, noticing Mary's troubled expression. "What's wrong?" he asked, his voice thick with sleep.

"I can't stop thinking about the house," Mary admitted. "It's like it's calling to me."

John wrapped his arms around her, trying to offer comfort. "We'll figure this out. But right now, we need to rest."

Lucy and Tom, in the adjoining room, were also finding sleep elusive. Lucy tossed and turned, haunted by nightmares of the shadows that had pursued her in the mansion. Tom lay awake, listening to the faint whispers that seemed to follow him even here.

The next morning, the family gathered for breakfast in the inn's small dining room. The air was thick with unspoken tension, and the innkeeper, sensing their unease, offered a sympathetic smile.

"Old Bartholomew's place has a way of getting under your skin," she said, placing a plate of eggs and bacon on the table. "You folks be careful. Some things are best left alone."

John and Mary exchanged worried glances. They knew they couldn't leave things as they were, but the thought of returning to the mansion filled them with dread. Still, they couldn't shake the feeling that they had unfinished business there.

"Maybe we should go back," Lucy suggested hesitantly. "Just to make sure we did everything right."

Tom nodded in agreement. "We can't let it win."

John sighed, realizing they had little choice. "Alright. We'll go back and make sure. But we need to be prepared."

They spent the day gathering supplies: candles, flashlights, and anything else they thought might help them navigate the mansion's dark corridors. As the sun set, they steeled themselves for the return journey.

The drive back to the mansion was filled with a sense of foreboding. The forest seemed darker, the trees leaning in as if to swallow them whole. When they finally reached the mansion, it stood silent and imposing, as if waiting for them.

John unlocked the front door, and they stepped inside, the air heavy with the scent of dust and decay. The familiar creaks and groans of the old house greeted them, and they knew that whatever presence they had encountered was still there.

The family decided to split up to cover more ground. John and Mary would search the first floor while Lucy and Tom headed upstairs to the attic. They hoped to find any clues they might have missed before.

John and Mary moved through the darkened halls, their flashlights casting eerie shadows on the walls. They revisited the library, the parlor, and the dining room, but found nothing new. The sense of being watched grew stronger with each passing moment, and Mary couldn't shake the feeling that something was following them.

Upstairs, Lucy and Tom approached the attic with trepidation. The narrow staircase creaked under their weight, and the air grew colder as they ascended. The attic was just as they remembered it—dim and cluttered, filled with old trunks and boxes.

"Let's start with the chest we found before," Lucy suggested, her voice barely above a whisper.

Tom nodded, and they made their way to the corner where the chest sat. As they opened it, the air grew even colder, and a faint whispering filled their ears. They sifted through the contents: old books, faded photographs, and strange artifacts. One book, in particular, caught Lucy's eye. It was bound in dark leather, with a symbol etched into the cover that she recognized from the journal they had found.

"This might be important," she said, showing the book to Tom.

As they examined the book, the whispering grew louder, more insistent. Lucy opened it, revealing pages filled with cryptic symbols and incantations. She tried to decipher the text, but it seemed to shift and change before her eyes.

Suddenly, the attic door slammed shut, plunging them into darkness. Tom's flashlight flickered and went out, leaving them in complete blackness. Panic set in, and they scrambled to find each other.

"Lucy, are you okay?" Tom called out, his voice trembling.

"I'm here," Lucy replied, her voice shaking. "We need to get out of here."

They fumbled their way back to the door, but it wouldn't budge. The whispering grew louder, and they felt a cold presence pressing in on them. Lucy clutched the book to her chest, hoping it might offer some protection.

Downstairs, John and Mary heard the commotion and rushed to the attic. They found the door locked and could hear their children's frantic cries.

"Tom! Lucy!" John shouted, pounding on the door. "Hold on, we're coming!"

Mary grabbed a nearby chair and used it to break down the door. The wood splintered under the impact, and they burst into the attic, finding Lucy and Tom huddled together, their faces pale with fear.

"We need to leave," Tom said, his voice shaking. "There's something up here."

John helped them to their feet, and they hurried downstairs, not stopping until they were back in the parlor. The house seemed to close in around them, the shadows growing darker and more oppressive.

"We need to figure out what's going on," Mary said, her voice resolute. "We can't just run away."

John nodded, taking the book from Lucy. "This might be the key. Let's see what we can learn."

As they pored over the book, the family felt a growing sense of urgency. The text was difficult to decipher, filled with symbols and incantations that seemed to shift and change. John and Mary worked together, trying to make sense of the cryptic writings.

"This seems to be a journal of sorts," John said, pointing to a passage. "Bartholomew was trying to harness dark powers, but he mentions something about a guardian spirit that protects the house."

Mary frowned. "A guardian spirit? Could that be what's causing all of this?"

"It's possible," John replied. "If Bartholomew summoned it, it might still be here, trying to protect the house from us."

They continued to read, and the pieces of the puzzle slowly began to come together. Bartholomew had conducted rituals to bind the guardian spirit to the mansion, hoping to use its power for his own ends. But something had gone wrong, and the spirit had become malevolent, trapping the souls of their ancestors and anyone else who entered the house.

"We need to find a way to release the spirit," Mary said. "That's the only way to end this."

As they discussed their plan, the house seemed to grow restless. The whispering voices returned, louder and more insistent, and the temperature dropped. The family felt a sense of impending doom, as if the house was preparing to strike.

"We need to stay together," John said, his voice firm. "No matter what happens, we can't let it separate us."

They gathered their supplies and prepared for the ritual. The instructions in the book were clear, but the process was complex and fraught with danger. They would need to perform the ritual in the heart of the mansion, in the library where Bartholomew had conducted his experiments.

The family moved cautiously through the darkened halls, their flashlights casting long shadows on the walls. The air was thick with tension, and every creak of the floorboards set their nerves on edge.

As they entered the library, the whispering grew louder, filling their ears with unintelligible murmurs. They set up their candles and arranged the items they needed for the ritual: a silver chalice, a piece of Isabella's portrait, and locks of hair from each family member.

John began to recite the incantation from the book, his voice steady despite the fear gnawing at his insides. The candles flickered, and the air grew colder, the shadows on the walls shifting and swirling.

Mary, Lucy, and Tom joined hands, their eyes closed in concentration. They could feel the presence of the guardian spirit, a cold, malevolent force pressing in on them from all sides.

As John spoke the final words of the incantation, a powerful gust of wind swept through the room, extinguishing the candles and plunging them into darkness. The whispering voices grew louder, more frenzied, and the family felt a suffocating pressure, as if the very walls were closing in on them.

"Hold on!" John shouted over the noise. "We're almost there!"

The room seemed to tilt, and they struggled to keep their balance. The shadows closed in, and they felt a cold, clammy presence wrap around them, squeezing the breath from their lungs.

Then, as abruptly as it began, the chaos stopped. The candles relit themselves, and the room returned to normal. The air was still, and the whispering voices were gone.

The family stood in stunned silence, their hearts racing as they looked around the now eerily quiet library. The shadows on the walls had returned to their normal, static forms, and the oppressive atmosphere seemed to lift, if only slightly.

The immediate danger seemed to have passed, but the family remained on edge. They examined the library carefully, searching for any signs that the ritual had worked. The air still felt heavy, and the whispers, though quieter, seemed to linger in the corners of their minds.

John and Mary sat down with the journal, trying to decipher the final passages. Lucy and Tom, though exhausted and shaken, kept a watchful eye on the surroundings, their nerves frayed from the recent experience.

"It's like the house is holding its breath," Lucy said, her voice barely above a whisper. "Waiting for something."

John nodded, his brow furrowed in concentration. "The book mentioned that the guardian spirit was bound by Bartholomew's rituals. If we've released it, it might need time to... settle."

Mary looked around the library, noticing that some of the books had shifted during the ritual. She approached the bookshelf and began to rearrange the disheveled volumes. As she moved a large tome, she felt a strange chill. The room seemed to darken momentarily, and she caught a glimpse of something—a shadowy figure—out of the corner of her eye.

"John, do you see that?" Mary asked, her voice trembling.

John turned to look, but the figure was gone. "What did you see?"

Mary shook her head. "Never mind. It's probably just my imagination."

They continued their search, but the sense of unease grew stronger. The mansion's oppressive silence was occasionally broken by faint creaks and groans, as if the house itself was protesting their intrusion.

As they worked, Tom noticed something peculiar about the portrait of Isabella. The eyes seemed to follow him, and the expression on her face appeared to shift, from stern to sorrowful. He pointed it out to his parents, who exchanged worried glances.

"Maybe it's just a trick of the light," John said, though he wasn't entirely convinced.

The family decided to take a break and rest in the parlor. They settled into the worn-out chairs, trying to relax, but the tension in the air was palpable. The fireplace crackled softly, its warmth a small comfort against the encroaching cold.

Suddenly, a loud thud echoed from the second floor. The family jumped, their hearts racing. John and Mary exchanged worried glances.

"Let's check it out," John said, standing up. "We need to be sure everything is okay."

The family climbed the stairs, their footsteps heavy with trepidation. As they reached the second floor, they saw that the hallway was eerily quiet. The doors to the bedrooms stood slightly ajar, and the air was thick with a sense of foreboding.

They approached the master bedroom, where the noise seemed to have originated. The door was slightly open, and John pushed it gently. The room was dimly lit by the moonlight streaming through the window. The bed was neatly made, but something was amiss.

On the floor, they found a broken vase. It had fallen from a shelf, its contents scattered across the floor. The family's sense of dread deepened. The vase was an old family heirloom, and its destruction felt like a bad omen.

Mary knelt to pick up the pieces, her hands trembling. "This must have happened during the commotion earlier. But why would it fall now?"

John frowned. "It doesn't make sense. There's something we're missing."

As they cleaned up the mess, the temperature in the room dropped abruptly. A cold breeze swept through, causing the curtains to flutter. The family felt an icy chill, and the whispering voices returned, more insistent than before.

"It's like it's getting worse," Lucy said, her voice shaking. "We need to do something."

John and Mary decided to perform another round of the ritual, hoping to solidify their efforts. They returned to the parlor and gathered the items they needed: the journal, the candles, and the artifacts. As they prepared, they noticed that the mansion seemed to react. The air grew colder, and the whispers grew louder, echoing off the walls.

The family gathered in the parlor once more, determined to complete the ritual and put an end to the disturbances. John lit the candles and arranged them in a circle, while Mary set out the items according to the instructions in the journal.

John began reciting the incantations, his voice steady but laced with tension. The flickering candlelight cast eerie shadows on the walls, and the temperature in the room dropped further. The whispers grew louder, forming a cacophony of voices that seemed to press in on them from all sides.

As John spoke the final words of the incantation, a powerful gust of wind swept through the room, extinguishing the candles and plunging them into darkness. The family clung to each other, their breaths visible in the freezing air.

The shadows on the walls twisted and danced, taking on grotesque shapes. The whispering voices became a roar, a thunderous cacophony that filled their ears and minds. The pressure in the room intensified, making it difficult to breathe.

"We have to hold on!" John shouted, his voice barely audible over the din. "We're almost there!"

Mary tightened her grip on Lucy and Tom, her eyes wide with fear. The shadows seemed to reach out for them, their cold fingers brushing against their skin. The house itself felt alive, its walls pulsing with a dark, malevolent energy.

The family stood together, focusing on the incantation and trying to block out the overwhelming fear. The shadows writhed and twisted, the whispers growing louder and more frantic.

Then, as suddenly as it had started, the chaos stopped. The wind ceased, the temperature returned to normal, and the whispering voices fell silent. The room was still, the shadows now calm and static.

The family looked around, their faces pale and exhausted. The candles relit themselves, casting a warm glow over the room. The oppressive atmosphere had lifted, and the sense of dread seemed to dissipate.

"We did it," Mary said, her voice trembling with relief. "I think it's over."

John nodded, though he remained wary. "We need to be sure. Let's stay here for a while and see if anything changes."

The family spent the rest of the night in the parlor, keeping a close watch on their surroundings. The mansion remained quiet, its oppressive atmosphere seemingly lifted. They hoped that the ritual had succeeded in breaking the curse and freeing the spirits trapped within the house.

As dawn approached, they felt a sense of cautious optimism. The mansion's dark grip seemed to have loosened, and the family began to relax. They knew they had faced something terrifying and had emerged stronger, but the memory of their ordeal would linger.

As the days went by, the Davis family began to believe that the worst was behind them. They spent their time exploring the mansion, trying to make it more livable and less frightening. They cleaned the dust from the furniture, repaired broken windows, and even started to make plans for renovations.

However, their sense of peace was short-lived. Strange occurrences began to crop up once more. At first, it was small things—objects moving on their own, creaks in the floorboards, and inexplicable cold spots. But soon, the disturbances grew more intense and unsettling.

One night, as Lucy was studying in her room, she heard a soft, rhythmic tapping on the window. She looked up, but there was no one outside. The tapping continued, growing louder and more insistent. Lucy went to the window and peered out, but saw only the dark, empty forest.

She turned back to her desk, trying to ignore the tapping, but it was relentless. The tapping turned into scratching, and Lucy could feel her heart pounding in her chest. She grabbed a flashlight and opened the window, but there was nothing there.

Tom, hearing the commotion, came to check on her. "What's going on?"

"I heard something outside," Lucy said, her voice trembling. "It was like scratching on the window."

Tom looked out into the dark forest, but saw nothing. "Maybe it was just an animal."

Lucy wasn't convinced, and the sense of unease lingered. That night, she had trouble sleeping, her mind racing with thoughts of the mansion's dark history and the malevolent forces that had once resided within.

Meanwhile, Mary and John experienced their own disturbances. Mary woke in the middle of the night to find her bedroom door slightly ajar. She heard faint, ghostly whispers and saw shadows moving across the walls. She tried to calm herself, telling herself it was just her imagination, but the whispers continued, growing louder and more frantic.

John, too, felt the weight of the mansion's dark presence. He would often hear footsteps echoing through the halls, even though no one else was around. The house seemed to be alive with activity, its dark energy seeping into every corner.

One evening, as the family sat in the parlor, a sudden, violent storm rolled in. The wind howled through the trees, and the rain battered against the windows. The mansion groaned and creaked, its old timbers straining against the storm's fury.

As the storm raged outside, the house seemed to come alive with its own dark energy. The lights flickered, casting eerie shadows on the walls. The whispering voices returned, louder than ever, filling the room with a sense of dread.

John and Mary gathered the children and tried to reassure them. "It's just a storm," John said, though his voice betrayed his own anxiety. "We're safe here."

But the storm seemed to stir something within the mansion. The shadows on the walls grew darker and more menacing, and the whispers turned into anguished wails. The family huddled together, their fear palpable.

Suddenly, a loud crash came from the attic. The family jumped, their hearts racing. John grabbed a flashlight and led the way upstairs, the others following closely behind.

When they reached the attic, they found that the old chest had been thrown across the room, its contents scattered. The attic was filled with an oppressive darkness, and the air was thick with a sense of malevolence.

"This is just like before," Mary said, her voice trembling. "We need to figure out what's causing this."

John nodded. "Let's check the journal again. Maybe there's something we missed."

They returned to the parlor and resumed their study of the journal. As they read through the cryptic passages, they discovered a section about the mansion's history. It detailed the dark rituals performed by Bartholomew and mentioned a final incantation to banish the guardian spirit once and for all.

"The final incantation," John said, his eyes widening. "It might be our last chance to end this."

The family prepared for the ritual, gathering the necessary items and setting up the room. They knew it would be dangerous, but they were determined to put an end to the haunting once and for all.

As they performed the ritual, the mansion seemed to react violently. The shadows grew darker, the whispers louder, and the temperature dropped. The family struggled to hold their ground, their fear mounting with each passing moment.

But despite the chaos, they pressed on. John recited the incantation with unwavering determination, while Mary and the children focused on the ritual, their fear giving way to resolve.

After what felt like an eternity, the ritual reached its climax. The shadows on the walls writhed and twisted, the whispers turned into a deafening roar, and the pressure in the room intensified.

And then, as suddenly as it began, the chaos stopped. The shadows receded, the whispers fell silent, and the temperature returned to normal. The room was still, and the oppressive atmosphere seemed to lift.

The family stood together, their faces pale and exhausted. They had faced the darkness once more, and this time, they hoped they had finally broken the mansion's grip.

As they prepared to leave the mansion, a final whisper echoed through the room, chilling them to the bone: "Thank you... but beware. The darkness is never truly gone."

The family left the mansion, their hearts heavy with the knowledge that they had faced something truly terrifying. They vowed to stay together and protect each other, knowing that the battle against darkness was never truly over.

The Davis family left the mansion, their minds and hearts weighed down by their harrowing experiences. The mansion, though silent, seemed to watch them leave with an almost malevolent satisfaction.

As they drove away, the forest around the mansion seemed to exhale, the oppressive atmosphere lifting slightly. They had survived the ordeal, but the scars—both physical and emotional—would remain with them forever.

They moved to a new home, far from the mansion's dark shadow. Their new house, though modest, felt like a sanctuary compared to the mansion. They slowly began to rebuild their lives, trying to put the horrors of the past behind them.

John and Mary sought counseling to help process their traumatic experiences. The children, Lucy and Tom, struggled with nightmares and anxiety but found solace in their new environment and the support of their family.

As the years passed, the Davis family found a measure of peace. They occasionally thought of the mansion and the darkness they had faced, but they chose to focus on the present and the future.

But the mansion's legacy was not easily forgotten. On quiet, stormy nights, they would sometimes hear faint whispers carried on the wind. The memory of the mansion remained a shadow in their minds, a reminder of the darkness they had confronted.

They continued to honor the lessons they had learned in the mansion, staying close as a family and cherishing their time together. They knew that the darkness might never be fully vanquished, but they were determined to face it together, no matter what.

The mansion remained abandoned, a silent sentinel in the woods, waiting for the next chapter in its dark history. But for the Davis family, their story was one of survival and strength, a testament to their courage in the face of unimaginable fear.

CHAPTER 5: THE WHISPERING SHADOWS

The Davis family settled into their new home, hoping to find solace and normalcy far from the haunted mansion. The house was modest but cozy, surrounded by a well-tended garden and nestled in a peaceful neighborhood. Yet, despite the change in scenery, the unsettling events from their past seemed to linger in their minds, casting a shadow over their attempts to rebuild their lives.

One evening, as Mary prepared dinner in the kitchen, she noticed a strange chill in the air. She dismissed it as a draft from the old windows and continued with her cooking. However, the feeling of being watched persisted, growing stronger as the days went by.

The children, Lucy and Tom, had started to adjust to their new school, but they couldn't shake the nightmares that plagued their sleep. Tom often woke in the middle of the night, convinced he heard footsteps in the hallways.

Lucy experienced vivid dreams of the mansion's dark corridors and the shadowy figures that haunted them.

One night, as Lucy lay in bed, she heard a soft whispering. At first, she thought it was just the wind or the old house settling, but the whispers grew louder and more insistent. They seemed to come from the shadows in her room, curling around her like a cold, invisible presence.

Lucy sat up in bed, her heart pounding. The whispers seemed to form words, though they were too garbled to make out. She tried to call out for her parents, but her voice was caught in her throat. The room grew colder, and the shadows on the walls danced and shifted.

Suddenly, the whispers stopped, and the room was filled with an eerie silence. Lucy turned on her bedside lamp, but the light flickered and then went out. She was left in the darkness, her fear growing with each passing second.

In the kitchen, Mary felt a cold breeze brush against her neck. She turned, but there was no one there. She tried to ignore it and continued preparing dinner. However, the feeling of being watched was overwhelming, and she couldn't shake the sense of unease.

She went to the living room, where John was reading a book. "John, have you noticed anything strange lately?" she asked, her voice tinged with worry.

John looked up from his book, his brow furrowed. "What do you mean?"

"I don't know," Mary said, her voice trembling. "It's just... I feel like something's wrong. Like there's something watching us."

John sighed, setting his book aside. "We've been through a lot. Maybe it's just the stress. We need to focus on settling in and moving forward."

Mary nodded, though she wasn't entirely convinced. She couldn't shake the feeling that something from their past was following them, haunting their new home.

As the days passed, the feeling of unease in the house grew stronger. The family tried to ignore it, focusing on unpacking and making their new home comfortable. Yet, strange occurrences became more frequent and unsettling.

One morning, as John was preparing breakfast, he noticed that the kitchen utensils were out of place. The silverware drawer was open, and the knives were arranged in an unusual pattern. He assumed it was just his own absent-mindedness and put everything back in its place.

Later that day, while cleaning the attic, Mary found an old box that had been left behind. Inside were various items: old photographs, letters, and a faded journal. Curious, she began to examine the contents, hoping to learn more about the previous occupants of the house.

The journal was filled with mundane entries about daily life, but one entry caught Mary's eye. It was a cryptic note about strange occurrences and unsettling feelings. The writer mentioned hearing whispers and seeing shadows in the corners of their vision. The entry ended with a warning: "Beware the shadows that linger."

Mary's heart raced as she read the note. It mirrored the feelings she had been experiencing in their new home. She decided to show the journal to John, hoping it might provide some answers.

That evening, as John read the journal, the whispers returned. They filled the house, echoing through the rooms. John and Mary tried to dismiss them as their imagination, but the sounds grew louder and more persistent.

In the middle of the night, Tom woke to find his bedroom door slightly ajar. He could hear faint, ghostly whispers coming from the hallway. He got out of bed and crept to the door, but saw nothing. The whispers seemed to be coming from everywhere and nowhere at once.

Tom's fear grew, and he rushed to Lucy's room. He found her awake, her eyes wide with terror. "Do you hear that?" he asked, his voice trembling.

Lucy nodded, her face pale. "Yes, it's like there's something here with us."

They huddled together, trying to comfort each other. The whispers continued, growing louder and more insistent. The shadows in the hallway seemed to move, their shapes shifting and changing.

The following day, John and Mary decided to investigate the history of the house. They visited the local library and searched through old records and newspapers. They discovered that the house had a long history of unusual occurrences and mysterious events.

One article detailed a series of strange incidents involving the previous occupants. They had reported hearing whispers, seeing shadows, and experiencing unexplained cold spots. The article ended with a chilling note: "The house seems to have a life of its own, feeding off the fear of its inhabitants."

John and Mary's unease grew as they read the article. It seemed that their new home had a dark history, one that echoed the experiences they had in the mansion.

Determined to understand what was happening, John and Mary sought the help of a local historian who specialized in haunted houses. They met with her in a small café, hoping she could shed light on the house's dark history.

The historian, a middle-aged woman named Evelyn, listened intently as John and Mary described their experiences. She nodded sympathetically and explained that some houses seemed to be "haunted" due to residual energies or events that had taken place within their walls.

"Sometimes, these energies are linked to the fears and anxieties of the people who live there," Evelyn said. "They can create a sort of feedback loop, intensifying the disturbances."

John and Mary listened closely as Evelyn continued. "In some cases, houses have a sort of residual energy from past events, or even from the people who lived there before. It's like an echo that persists long after the original events have passed."

Evelyn suggested they perform a cleansing ritual to try to dispel any lingering energies. She provided them with instructions and a list of items they would need: sage, salt, and a bowl of water.

Back at the house, John and Mary prepared for the ritual. They gathered the items and followed Evelyn's instructions, lighting the sage and sprinkling salt in the corners of each room. As they worked, the house seemed to respond, the temperature dropping and the whispers growing louder.

The ritual seemed to have a brief calming effect. The oppressive atmosphere lifted momentarily, and the house felt quieter. However, the sense of unease soon returned, and the whispers started again, now more insistent and urgent.

As night fell, the disturbances grew more intense. The shadows on the walls seemed to move and shift, and the temperature dropped dramatically. The family huddled together in the living room, trying to ignore the unsettling occurrences.

Suddenly, a loud crash came from the basement. John and Mary exchanged worried glances and decided to investigate. They grabbed flashlights and made their way down the dark stairs.

The basement was cold and damp, filled with old boxes and forgotten furniture. The crash had come from a fallen shelf, and the items it had held were scattered across the floor. John and Mary carefully picked up the items, trying to make sense of the mess.

As they worked, they noticed something unusual: a small, old-fashioned key lying among the debris. It was ornate and seemed to have an intricate design. John picked it up, feeling a chill run down his spine.

"What do you think this is for?" Mary asked, her voice trembling.

"I don't know," John said. "But it might be worth looking into."

The discovery of the key added to the growing sense of mystery surrounding their new home. John and Mary decided to investigate further, hoping that the key might unlock some answers about the house's dark history.

They searched the house, looking for any lock or door that the key might fit. Their search led them to a small, forgotten room in the attic. It had been sealed off and was filled with dust and cobwebs.

John inserted the key into the lock, and with a click, the door creaked open. Inside, they found an old trunk covered in dust. The trunk was bound with rusty metal straps and had an intricate lock that matched the key.

With a mixture of excitement and trepidation, John unlocked the trunk. Inside, they discovered a collection of old documents, photographs, and a leather-bound book. The documents were yellowed with age, and the photographs depicted the house and its previous occupants.

The book was filled with handwritten notes and sketches. It appeared to be a personal diary, documenting the experiences of the house's previous residents. The entries described strange occurrences, such as shadowy figures, disembodied voices, and unexplained cold spots.

One entry in particular caught their attention. It detailed a ritual performed by the house's previous owner, who had attempted to harness the house's dark energy for their own purposes. The entry ended with a warning: "The darkness cannot be controlled. It will consume all who seek to master it."

John and Mary's unease deepened as they read the diary. It seemed that their new home had a long history of dark rituals and malevolent forces.

As they continued to explore the trunk, they discovered a small, ornate box hidden among the documents. The box was locked, and John noticed that it had no keyhole. Instead, it had a series of strange symbols engraved on its surface.

Mary examined the symbols closely. "These look like some of the symbols from the journal," she said. "Maybe they're part of the ritual we performed."

They decided to consult Evelyn once more, hoping she could provide insight into the symbols and the box. They arranged to meet with her the following day.

Evelyn examined the symbols on the box and the diary's entries with great interest. She explained that the symbols were part of an ancient occult ritual, designed to bind or control dark entities. The box, she speculated, might contain an object of significant power or a key to understanding the house's dark energy.

"The ritual described in the diary suggests that the previous owner was trying to control the house's dark forces,"

Evelyn said. "It's possible that the box contains something related to those efforts."

John and Mary were eager to learn more, but Evelyn cautioned them. "Be careful. The forces at play here are not to be taken lightly. If the box contains something dangerous, it's best to handle it with extreme caution."

With Evelyn's guidance, John and Mary decided to open the box carefully. They gathered in the living room, the atmosphere tense with anticipation. John used a small tool to pry open the box, revealing its contents.

Inside, they found an old, worn amulet. It was intricately designed, with a dark gemstone at its center. The amulet emitted a faint, eerie glow, and the air around it seemed to grow colder.

John and Mary examined the amulet, feeling a sense of unease. Evelyn explained that the amulet was likely used in the ritual to channel or amplify the house's dark energy. It could be a source of great power or great danger.

"It's important to understand what you're dealing with," Evelyn said. "If you decide to keep the amulet, be cautious. It might have lingering effects on the house's energy."

John and Mary decided to keep the amulet, hoping that it might help them understand and control the dark forces within the house. They returned to their home, determined to find a way to neutralize the malevolent energy that seemed to haunt them.

Despite their best efforts, the whispers and shadows continued to plague the Davis family. The house seemed to have a life of its own, reacting to their attempts to understand and control its dark energy.

One evening, as the family gathered for dinner, the atmosphere grew heavy with unease. The shadows on the walls seemed to move, and the temperature in the room dropped abruptly.

The whispers returned, filling the room with a sense of dread. John and Mary exchanged worried glances, knowing that their efforts to rid the house of its dark energy had not succeeded.

The amulet, though carefully stored, seemed to exert a powerful influence on the house. The family could feel its presence, a constant reminder of the darkness they had encountered.

As the days turned into weeks, the disturbances became more frequent and intense. The shadows grew darker, the whispers louder, and the cold spots more pronounced. The family's sense of peace was overshadowed by the lingering presence of the dark forces within the house.

John and Mary decided to consult Evelyn once more, hoping she could provide guidance on how to neutralize the amulet's influence. They hoped that with her help, they could finally put an end to the haunting and find a measure of peace.

The journey to understand and control the darkness was far from over, but the Davis family remained determined to face the challenges ahead. They knew that the house's dark history and the malevolent forces that lingered within were formidable adversaries, but they were resolute in their commitment to confronting the shadows and reclaiming their home.

CHAPTER 6: THE HAUNTING INTENSIFIES

The Davis family had hoped that the arrival of summer would bring a sense of normalcy and respite from the eerie occurrences that plagued their home. Instead, the oppressive atmosphere seemed to settle deeper into the fabric of their lives, suffusing their days with a growing sense of dread.

One warm summer evening, John and Mary decided to host a small barbecue in their backyard. They hoped the distraction of friends and the joy of socializing might lift their spirits and bring some semblance of normalcy to their lives. The children, Lucy and Tom, eagerly invited their new friends over, hoping to forget the shadows and whispers that haunted their nights.

As the sun dipped below the horizon and the first stars appeared, the backyard was filled with the comforting sounds of laughter and conversation. The smell of grilled meat and fresh vegetables wafted through the air, mingling with the scent of blooming flowers. For a brief moment, the Davis family felt a sense of peace.

However, as the night progressed, the atmosphere grew increasingly unsettling. The temperature seemed to drop suddenly, and an eerie silence settled over the yard. The laughter and chatter of the guests grew quieter, and the darkness seemed to press in around them.

John and Mary exchanged worried glances as the temperature continued to fall. The once-warm evening turned cold, and a chill swept through the gathering. The guests began to shiver and murmur about the sudden change in weather.

Lucy and Tom's friends looked around, their faces reflecting the same unease that had settled over their hosts. The shadows cast by the porch lights seemed to move and shift, and the once-friendly darkness of the evening took on a menacing quality.

The first sign of trouble came when one of Lucy's friends, Sarah, let out a frightened squeal. She had noticed a shadowy figure standing near the edge of the yard, partially obscured by the trees. The figure seemed to watch them with an intense, malevolent gaze.

John quickly reassured the guests, trying to dispel their fears. He suggested that it was just a trick of the light and encouraged everyone to enjoy the rest of the evening. However, the sense of unease persisted, and the guests began to leave one by one, their cheerful demeanor replaced by anxious glances over their shoulders.

As the last of the guests departed, John and Mary were left alone with their children. The atmosphere was heavy with silence, and the oppressive presence that had marked their previous encounters seemed to return with a vengeance.

The family retreated inside, hoping to escape the unsettling atmosphere of the backyard. However, the house seemed to respond to their unease. The lights flickered and dimmed, and the temperature continued to drop.

John and Mary decided to check the house's electrical system, hoping to identify any issues. They ventured into the basement, where the temperature was even colder and the air felt thick with an unsettling energy.

As they inspected the circuit breaker, a sudden, loud bang echoed through the basement. The noise came from the far corner of the room, where an old trunk had fallen over. John and Mary exchanged worried glances and approached the trunk.

Inside, they found various old tools and dusty items. Among them was a collection of old newspapers and a strange, small box. The box was intricately decorated, with symbols similar to those they had seen before.

The temperature in the basement dropped even further as they examined the box. The air grew colder, and the whispers from before seemed to return, growing louder and more insistent.

The discovery of the box in the basement added to the growing sense of unease within the Davis household. John and Mary decided to keep the box in a safe place while they continued to investigate its significance. They hoped that by understanding its origins, they might find a way to neutralize the lingering presence that haunted their home.

The next few days were marked by an increasing intensity of the haunting. The house seemed to be alive with a dark, malevolent energy. The whispers grew louder and more coherent, often forming chilling phrases that echoed through the empty rooms.

One night, as the family settled into bed, they heard a series of disorienting noises. The sound of footsteps echoed through the hallway, growing louder and more erratic. The footsteps seemed to be moving closer to their bedrooms, accompanied by an unsettling scraping sound.

John and Mary, already on edge, decided to investigate. They ventured into the hallway, their flashlights casting long, flickering shadows on the walls. The temperature in the corridor was icy, and the oppressive atmosphere made it difficult to breathe.

As they searched the hallway, they found nothing out of the ordinary. The sounds had ceased, leaving only the eerie silence of the house. They returned to their bedrooms, but sleep proved elusive. The whispers continued, their voices rising and falling in a haunting melody.

In the middle of the night, Tom woke up to find his room filled with a thick, black fog. The fog seemed to coalesce into dark shapes that moved and shifted around him. Tom tried to call out for his parents, but his voice was swallowed by the oppressive darkness.

Lucy, in the adjacent room, was also disturbed by the fog. She saw the dark shapes pressing against her window, their shadowy forms distorting the light from outside. The whispers grew louder, their voices a cacophony of fear and despair.

The children huddled together, trying to comfort each other. They could feel the coldness of the fog seeping through the walls and the floor. The shadows seemed to reach out for them, their presence a tangible, suffocating force.

The next morning, John and Mary noticed the effects of the night's disturbances. The children were visibly shaken, and their dreams were filled with dark, unsettling imagery. The house's atmosphere was more oppressive than ever, with the shadows seeming to grow darker and more menacing.

John decided to investigate the box they had found in the basement. He examined it closely, trying to decipher the symbols and understand its purpose. He discovered that the box had a hidden compartment, which contained an old, weathered letter.

The letter was written in an ornate script and detailed a series of rituals performed by the house's previous occupants. The rituals were designed to harness or control dark forces, but the letter warned of the dangers of such practices. It described the dark forces as unpredictable and malevolent, capable of causing great harm to those who sought to control them.

The letter ended with a dire warning: "The darkness will never be fully contained. It will always seek to break free and consume those who dare to control it."

John and Mary were deeply disturbed by the letter. It seemed to confirm their fears that the house's dark forces were not easily controlled. They decided to consult Evelyn again, hoping she could provide guidance on how to address the escalating haunting.

Evelyn agreed to meet with John and Mary to discuss the findings from their investigation. They arranged to meet at her office, a small, cluttered space filled with books and artifacts related to the supernatural.

As they presented their findings, Evelyn listened attentively. She examined the symbols on the box and the letter with great interest, her face growing more serious with each passing moment.

"This is more complex than I initially thought," Evelyn said, her voice grave. "The symbols on the box and the rituals described in the letter suggest that the previous occupants were involved in some very dangerous practices. They were trying to harness dark forces that are not easily controlled."

She continued, "The dark forces within the house may have been awakened or amplified by the rituals performed. This could explain the increase in disturbances and the malevolent presence you've been experiencing."

Evelyn suggested that they perform a more comprehensive cleansing ritual to address the dark forces within the house. She provided John and Mary with additional items and instructions, including the use of holy water, candles, and protective charms.

The family returned home, determined to follow Evelyn's guidance and confront the darkness within their home. They prepared for the ritual, gathering the necessary items and setting up the house for the cleansing.

As they performed the ritual, the house responded with increased intensity. The temperature dropped dramatically, and the whispers grew louder, their voices a chaotic blend of fear and anger. The shadows on the walls seemed to writhe and twist, and the air felt thick with an oppressive energy.

Despite the chaos, John and Mary pressed on with the ritual. They recited the incantations and used the protective charms, hoping to dispel the dark forces and bring a sense of peace to their home.

As the ritual reached its climax, the house seemed to react violently. The shadows on the walls grew darker, the whispers turned into a deafening roar, and the temperature plummeted. The family struggled to maintain their focus, their fear mounting with each passing moment.

The final moments of the ritual were a chaotic blur. The house seemed to convulse with a violent energy, the shadows on the walls twisting and writhing as if in agony. The whispers reached a crescendo, their voices a chaotic, dissonant roar.

John and Mary clung to their resolve, their voices rising above the din as they recited the final incantations. The protective charms glowed faintly, casting an eerie light in the darkened rooms. The family's determination was palpable, their fear giving way to a resolute courage.

Suddenly, the chaos stopped. The shadows receded, the whispers fell silent, and the temperature began to rise. The oppressive atmosphere lifted, leaving the house in an eerie, unsettling calm.

The family stood together, their faces pale and exhausted. They had faced the darkness once more, and for the moment, it seemed to have retreated. The house felt different, though the sense of unease remained.

As they cleaned up after the ritual, the children seemed to find some comfort in the newfound calm. Their nightmares and fears subsided, though the memory of the haunting lingered. John and Mary hoped that their efforts had succeeded in dispelling the dark forces that had plagued their home.

In the days that followed, the house remained quieter, though the shadows and whispers occasionally returned. The family continued to experience unsettling occurrences, but they felt more prepared to face them.

John and Mary knew that their journey was far from over. The darkness within their home had not been fully vanquished, and they remained vigilant in their efforts to protect their family and understand the malevolent forces that lingered.

As the summer continued, the Davis family faced the challenges of their haunted home with a mix of fear and determination. They hoped that their efforts to confront the darkness would ultimately bring them the peace and safety they so desperately sought.

CHAPTER 7: ECHOES OF TERROR

The Davis family hoped that the cleansing ritual had brought them a reprieve from the dark forces that had plagued their home. For a brief time, their hopes seemed to be realized as the house felt calmer, and the disturbing occurrences seemed to lessen. The oppressive atmosphere had lifted, and the family was able to enjoy moments of relative normalcy.

The children, Lucy and Tom, began to settle into a more comfortable routine. They spent their days playing outside and attending summer activities, trying to put the haunting experiences behind them. John and Mary focused on making their home a sanctuary, investing in repairs and renovations that would improve their living conditions.

However, the respite was short-lived. The first sign of trouble came one evening when John noticed an unusual smell in the house. It was a musty, foul odor that seemed to emanate from the walls. He dismissed it as a problem with the house's old plumbing, but the smell persisted and grew stronger.

Mary also noticed strange changes in the house. The temperature fluctuated wildly, with sudden cold spots appearing in different rooms. The shadows on the walls seemed to move more frequently, and the whispers, though quieter, never fully disappeared.

One night, as John and Mary prepared for bed, they heard a series of unsettling noises coming from the attic. The noises were rhythmic and persistent, like someone—or something—was moving around up there. The sounds were accompanied by an eerie creaking, as if the floorboards were being disturbed.

John decided to investigate, grabbing a flashlight and heading up to the attic. The stairs creaked under his weight, and the air grew colder as he ascended. When he reached the attic, he found nothing out of place. The old furniture and boxes were undisturbed, and the noises had ceased.

As he turned to leave, he noticed something unusual—a faint, glowing light coming from behind a stack of old boxes. John approached cautiously, and the light flickered as he drew closer. It was coming from a small, ornate mirror that had been hidden among the boxes.

The mirror was old and ornate, with an intricate frame and a tarnished glass surface. The light seemed to emanate from within the mirror, casting eerie reflections on the attic walls. John examined it closely, but he found no visible source for the light.

Feeling a growing sense of unease, John decided to bring the mirror downstairs. Mary was waiting anxiously, and when she saw the mirror, her expression changed to one of concern.

"It's strange," Mary said, her voice trembling. "I've had a feeling that something was watching us. Maybe this mirror has something to do with it."

John and Mary decided to keep the mirror covered and stored away, hoping that it might help them understand the lingering presence in the house. The unsettling experiences continued, and the family's sense of normalcy was shattered once more.

The mirror remained covered and stored in the corner of the living room, but its presence seemed to influence the atmosphere of the house. The oppressive feeling returned, and the disturbances became more frequent and intense.

One night, Lucy and Tom were awakened by a series of loud bangs coming from the attic. The sounds were followed by a sudden burst of cold air that seeped into their rooms. They huddled together, their fear mounting as the noises continued.

John and Mary decided to investigate once more. They found the attic in disarray, with old boxes and furniture scattered across the floor. The mirror was still covered, but the air felt heavier and colder around it.

Mary decided to remove the cover from the mirror, hoping to understand its connection to the disturbances. As she uncovered the mirror, the room grew colder, and the shadows seemed to stretch and darken. The light from the mirror flickered, casting eerie reflections on the walls.

John and Mary cautiously examined the mirror. The reflections seemed to distort and warp, creating unsettling images and shapes. The mirror appeared to act as a portal to something darker, and the reflections seemed to move independently of their own.

As they watched, the mirror began to show scenes from the past. The reflections depicted shadowy figures moving through the house, their faces obscured by darkness. The scenes were accompanied by whispers and indistinct voices, adding to the sense of dread.

John and Mary were deeply disturbed by the mirror's reflections. It seemed to reveal hidden aspects of the house's dark history, showing glimpses of the malevolent forces that had once been present. The mirror appeared to hold a key to understanding the house's haunting.

They decided to consult Evelyn once more, hoping she could provide insight into the mirror's significance. Evelyn agreed to meet with them and examine the mirror, eager to help uncover its secrets.

Evelyn arrived at the Davis home with a mix of curiosity and caution. She examined the mirror carefully, her expression growing more serious as she observed the reflections and the eerie light that emanated from it.

"This mirror is more than just an old object," Evelyn said, her voice grave. "It seems to be a conduit for the dark forces that haunt this house. The reflections are showing you glimpses of the past, but they also reveal the lingering presence of those forces."

Evelyn explained that the mirror might have been used in the house's previous rituals or practices. It could have been an instrument for channeling or amplifying the dark energy, and its presence was likely contributing to the ongoing disturbances.

"The mirror is acting as a focal point for the house's dark energy," Evelyn said. "It's possible that it's drawing on the residual forces and intensifying the haunting. You'll need to address the mirror directly to alleviate the disturbances."

Evelyn suggested performing a cleansing ritual specifically for the mirror. She provided John and Mary with additional instructions and items, including specific incantations and protective symbols.

The family prepared for the ritual, gathering the necessary items and setting up a space for the cleansing. They placed the mirror in the center of the room and began the ritual, reciting the incantations and using the protective symbols as Evelyn had instructed.

As they performed the ritual, the atmosphere in the house grew tense. The mirror's reflections became more chaotic, showing disturbing images and scenes from the past. The whispers grew louder, and the temperature continued to drop.

Despite the chaos, John and Mary pressed on with the ritual. They focused on the mirror, hoping that their efforts would help neutralize its influence and dispel the dark energy that had accumulated.

As the ritual reached its climax, the mirror began to emit a blinding light. The shadows in the room seemed to writhe and twist, and the whispers turned into a deafening roar. The family struggled to maintain their focus, their fear mounting with each passing moment.

The final moments of the ritual were chaotic and intense. The mirror's light grew brighter, casting an eerie glow throughout the room. The shadows seemed to reach out, and the whispers turned into a cacophony of voices.

John and Mary continued to recite the incantations, their voices rising above the din. The protective symbols glowed faintly, casting a dim light in the darkness. The family's determination was palpable, their fear giving way to a resolute courage.

Suddenly, the mirror shattered. The glass exploded into fragments, scattering across the room. The intense light and the oppressive energy dissipated, leaving the room in a state of uneasy calm.

John and Mary surveyed the damage, their faces pale and their bodies trembling. The mirror's destruction had brought a temporary reprieve, but the sense of unease remained. The house felt different, but the lingering presence of the dark forces was still palpable.

The shattered pieces of the mirror were collected and disposed of. The family hoped that removing the mirror would help alleviate the disturbances, but they remained cautious and vigilant.

In the days that followed, the house continued to experience unsettling occurrences. The shadows seemed to move more erratically, and the whispers, though quieter, were still present. The sense of dread had not entirely dissipated, and the family remained on edge.

John and Mary continued to work on improving their home, hoping that their efforts would bring a sense of peace and stability. They focused on repairing the damage caused by the mirror and addressing any issues that arose.

Despite their efforts, the haunting seemed to persist. The house had a way of reminding them that the dark forces within were not easily vanquished. The family faced each day with a mixture of fear and determination, hoping to find a way to fully address the lingering presence and bring lasting peace to their home.

One evening, as the family prepared for bed, they heard a series of strange noises coming from the basement. The sounds were muffled and indistinct, but they seemed to be accompanied by a low, guttural growl.

John and Mary decided to investigate, hoping to understand the source of the disturbance. They grabbed flashlights and descended into the basement, their footsteps echoing in the cold, dark space.

The basement was filled with the familiar musty smell, and the air felt heavy with an unsettling energy. The noises grew louder as they approached the far corner of the room.

As they reached the corner, they found an old, rusted door that had been hidden behind a stack of boxes. The door was partially ajar, and the growling noises seemed to be coming from behind it.

John and Mary exchanged worried glances and decided to open the door. The hinges creaked as they pushed it open, revealing a small, dimly lit room. The room was filled with old, discarded furniture and debris.

In the center of the room was a large, ancient-looking chest. The chest was covered in dust and cobwebs, and it seemed to emit a faint, eerie glow.

John and Mary approached the chest cautiously. The growling noises had ceased, and the air felt colder than ever. They examined the chest, noting the strange symbols and markings etched into its surface.

As they opened the chest, they were met with a chilling sight. The chest was filled with old, tattered books and papers, along with a collection of strange, occult objects. The items appeared to be related to the house's dark history, and the sense of dread in the room grew stronger.

The discovery of the chest added to the growing sense of unease. The family realized that their efforts to understand and control the dark forces within the house were far from over. The lingering presence of the malevolent energy continued to affect their lives, and they remained determined to confront the darkness and reclaim their home.

The night ended with the family feeling more apprehensive than ever. The chest's contents and the strange noises in the basement reinforced the notion that the house held many secrets and dangers yet to be uncovered.

John and Mary knew that their journey to understand and control the darkness within their home was far from complete. They faced each day with a mixture of fear and determination, hoping that their efforts would eventually bring them the peace and safety they so desperately sought.

CHAPTER 8: THE AWAKENING

The summer days grew hotter, and the Davis family's sense of dread seemed to intensify with each passing week. Despite their best efforts to understand and neutralize the dark forces within their home, the malevolent presence continued to cast a shadow over their lives. The disturbances became more frequent and increasingly unsettling.

One night, as John and Mary sat in their living room, the house was filled with an oppressive silence. The air was heavy, and the temperature had dropped suddenly, creating an uncomfortable chill. The shadows on the walls seemed to grow darker, their shapes shifting and writhing.

Lucy and Tom had gone to bed early, trying to escape the unsettling atmosphere that had pervaded their home.

John and Mary were discussing their next steps when they heard a loud crash from the attic. The sound was followed by a series of disorienting noises—thumps, creaks, and a low, guttural growl.

John and Mary exchanged worried glances. They decided to investigate, their fear mounting with each step. They climbed the stairs to the attic, the air growing colder as they ascended.

When they reached the attic, they found a disturbing sight. The old boxes and furniture were scattered across the floor, and the mirror's shattered remains were now partially covered by a thick layer of dust. In the center of the room stood a dark, shadowy figure.

The figure appeared to be a woman, her form obscured by darkness. Her eyes glowed with an eerie light, and her presence exuded a palpable malevolence. John and Mary's fear intensified as the figure began to speak in a haunting, disembodied voice.

"You thought you could banish me," the figure said, her voice echoing through the attic. "You thought you could control the darkness, but it is not so easily contained."

John and Mary tried to speak, but their voices were swallowed by the overwhelming fear. The shadowy figure seemed to draw closer, her form becoming more defined. Her eyes glowed with a sinister light, and her presence was suffused with a dark, oppressive energy.

The figure raised her hand, and the temperature in the room dropped further. A swirling mist began to form around her, and the air grew colder. The whispers from before returned, their voices blending into a cacophony of fear and despair.

John and Mary struggled to maintain their composure. They attempted to confront the figure, but their words were lost in the oppressive atmosphere. The figure's malevolent presence seemed to exert a powerful influence, pushing them back.

Suddenly, the figure vanished, leaving the attic in an eerie, unsettling silence. The temperature slowly returned to normal, but the sense of dread lingered. John and Mary were left shaken, their resolve to confront the darkness strengthened but their fear deepened.

Part 2: The Haunting Escalates

The appearance of the shadowy figure marked the beginning of a new phase in the haunting. The disturbances became more frequent and intense, and the malevolent presence within the house seemed to grow stronger.

The next few nights were marked by a series of terrifying events. The whispers in the house grew louder and more coherent, often forming chilling phrases that echoed through the empty rooms. The shadows on the walls seemed to move more erratically, and the temperature fluctuations became more pronounced.

One night, Lucy and Tom were awakened by a series of loud bangs coming from their bedroom door. The door rattled violently, and a cold draft swept through the room. The children huddled together, their fear mounting as the noises continued.

John and Mary rushed to their children's rooms, their hearts pounding with fear. They found the children trembling under their covers, their faces pale and their eyes wide with terror.

"It's okay," Mary said, trying to comfort them. "We're here. Everything will be alright."

As John and Mary reassured the children, the noises in the house grew more intense. The bangs and rattles continued, and the whispers became a deafening roar. The shadows in the hallway seemed to stretch and twist, their shapes taking on menacing forms.

John and Mary decided to investigate the source of the disturbances. They searched the house, but found nothing out of the ordinary. The temperature was cold, and the oppressive atmosphere seemed to follow them wherever they went.

As they explored, they encountered a series of unsettling phenomena. Doors creaked open and shut on their own, objects moved seemingly of their own accord, and the whispers seemed to follow them through the house.

The disturbances reached a climax one night when the family experienced a series of terrifying apparitions. Lucy and Tom saw ghostly figures moving through the hallways, their faces obscured by darkness. The figures appeared to be trapped, their expressions reflecting a sense of despair.

John and Mary saw similar apparitions, their forms more defined and menacing. The figures seemed to reach out to them, their eyes glowing with an eerie light. The apparitions' presence was accompanied by a powerful, oppressive energy that made it difficult to breathe.

The family's fear was palpable as they faced these unsettling encounters. They tried to remain calm and focused, but the intensity of the haunting made it increasingly difficult to maintain their composure.

As the haunting intensified, John and Mary decided to investigate the house's history further. They hoped to uncover more information about the dark forces within the house and the connection to the shadowy figure they had encountered.

They returned to the trunk they had discovered earlier, examining the old books and documents for any clues. The items in the trunk were related to occult practices and dark rituals, and John and Mary hoped to find answers that would help them understand the malevolent presence in their home.

Among the documents was an old, weathered book that detailed a series of rituals and ceremonies. The book included descriptions of various dark practices, including summoning and binding rituals. The rituals were accompanied by detailed illustrations and instructions, many of which were similar to the symbols they had seen before.

One particular section of the book caught John and Mary's attention. It described a ritual known as the "Witches' Gathering," which involved summoning and binding powerful entities. The ritual was said to be highly dangerous and could result in the entities gaining control over the summoner.

The book included detailed instructions for performing the ritual, along with warnings about the potential consequences. It described how the ritual could open a portal to the dark realm, allowing malevolent entities to enter the physical world.

John and Mary were alarmed by the similarities between the ritual described in the book and the experiences they had been having. They realized that the shadowy figure they had encountered might be one of the entities summoned by the previous occupants.

Determined to learn more, John and Mary continued to investigate. They researched the history of the house and its previous occupants, hoping to uncover any additional information that might help them understand the dark forces at play.

The Davis family's investigation led them to uncover a disturbing connection between the house's dark history and the witch they had encountered. The witch appeared to be a central figure in the house's malevolent presence, and her rituals seemed to have a significant impact on the haunting.

John and Mary discovered that the witch had been a practitioner of dark magic, using her powers to summon and control malevolent entities. The rituals she performed were designed to bind these entities to the house, creating a powerful and dangerous connection.

The family decided to confront the witch directly, hoping to break the hold she had on their home. They planned a ritual to banish the witch and the dark entities she had summoned.

As they prepared for the ritual, the atmosphere in the house grew tense. The temperature dropped, and the shadows on the walls seemed to grow darker. The whispers grew louder, their voices blending into a chaotic cacophony.

John and Mary set up the ritual space in the living room, placing protective symbols and items around the room. They recited the incantations and performed the necessary steps to prepare for the confrontation.

As the ritual began, the house responded with increased intensity. The shadows on the walls seemed to writhe and twist, and the temperature continued to drop. The whispers turned into a deafening roar, and the air felt thick with an oppressive energy.

The witch's presence became more pronounced as the ritual progressed. Her shadowy form appeared in the room, her eyes glowing with a sinister light. She spoke in a haunting, disembodied voice, taunting the family and challenging their efforts.

John and Mary pressed on with the ritual, their fear mounting as they faced the witch's malevolent presence. They continued to recite the incantations and perform the necessary steps, hoping that their efforts would be enough to banish the witch and the dark entities.

As the ritual reached its climax, the witch's form began to waver and distort. The shadows in the room grew darker, and the oppressive energy intensified. The family struggled to maintain their focus, their fear and exhaustion taking their toll.

As the ritual reached its peak, the witch's form seemed to dissolve into a swirling vortex of shadows. The air grew colder, and the oppressive energy in the room reached its zenith. John and Mary's voices were strained and desperate as they recited the final incantations.

Suddenly, the witch's malevolent presence surged, and the room was filled with a blinding light. The shadows writhed and twisted violently, and the temperature plummeted. The family was overwhelmed by a powerful, suffocating force.

In the midst of the chaos, the witch's voice echoed through the room, her words filled with rage and hatred. "You cannot escape the darkness," she said. "It is part of you, and it will consume you."

The blinding light began to fade, and the oppressive energy gradually lifted. The shadows on the walls grew less intense, and the temperature slowly returned to normal. The witch's presence seemed to dissipate, leaving the room in an uneasy calm.

John and Mary were left shaken and exhausted, their bodies trembling from the ordeal. They had confronted the witch and attempted to banish her, but the lingering sense of malevolence remained.

The house was quieter, but the darkness was far from gone. The family knew that their efforts had not fully resolved the haunting, and they remained vigilant in their efforts to understand and confront the dark forces within their home.

As the night ended, the Davis family faced an uncertain future. The haunting had reached new heights of terror, and the witch's presence had left a lasting mark on their lives. They knew that their journey to reclaim their home was far from over, and they prepared to face the darkness with a mixture of fear and determination.

CHAPTER 9: THE DESCENT INTO DARKNESS

THE FOLLOWING DAY, JOHN AND MARY DECIDE TO DELVE DEEPER INTO THE HOUSE'S HISTORY. THEY HOPED THAT UNCOVERING MORE INFORMATION ABOUT ITS PAST OCCUPANTS AND THEIR CONNECTIONS TO THE DARK FORCES MIGHT PROVIDE CLUES ON HOW TO FULLY ADDRESS THE HAUNTING.

They spent hours researching old records, newspapers, and property deeds, searching for any information related to the witch and the rituals performed in the house. Their investigation led them to discover unsettling details about the previous occupants.

The house had a long and troubling history, with numerous reports of strange occurrences and unexplained phenomena. The previous occupants had experienced similar disturbances, and some had even been driven to madness by the malevolent forces within the house.

Among the records, John and Mary found a series of newspaper articles detailing a series of tragic events that had occurred in the house. The articles described disappearances, mysterious deaths, and reports of a dark, shadowy figure that had been seen in the vicinity.

One particular article caught their attention. It described the house as a place of dark rituals and occult practices, with the previous occupants being involved in a series of malevolent ceremonies. The article mentioned a group of individuals who had practiced dark magic and had been rumored to summon powerful entities.

The discovery of these articles only deepened the family's sense of dread. The house's dark history seemed to be more sinister than they had initially realized. The malevolent presence within the house appeared to be a part of a much larger and more disturbing legacy.

As John and Mary continued their research, they began to piece together a clearer picture of the house's dark past. The witch they had encountered was not an isolated entity but part of a larger network of dark forces that had plagued the house for years.

The unsettling realization that their home was a focal point for dark rituals and malevolent entities added a new layer of fear to their already harrowing experiences. The house seemed to be a conduit for dark forces, and the family was determined to uncover the truth and find a way to banish the darkness once and for all.

As the days passed, the Davis family's experiences grew increasingly terrifying. The disturbances within the house became more frequent and intense, and the malevolent presence seemed to grow stronger.

One night, Lucy and Tom were awakened by a series of horrifying nightmares. They dreamed of shadowy figures moving through their rooms, their faces twisted in anguish. The dreams were accompanied by an overwhelming sense of dread, and the children woke up screaming.

John and Mary tried to comfort their children, but the nightmares continued. The children's fear began to affect their daily lives, and their once-happy demeanor was replaced by a constant state of anxiety.

The disturbances extended beyond the children's nightmares. The house seemed to come alive with malevolent energy, and the family experienced a series of frightening encounters. Objects moved on their own, doors slammed shut, and the shadows on the walls took on menacing forms.

One night, John and Mary were awakened by a series of loud, disorienting noises. The sounds were accompanied by a powerful, oppressive energy that filled the house. The temperature dropped suddenly, and the whispers grew louder, their voices blending into a chaotic cacophony.

John and Mary decided to investigate the source of the disturbances. They searched the house, but found nothing out of the ordinary. The atmosphere was thick with fear, and the oppressive energy seemed to follow them wherever they went.

As they explored, they encountered a series of unsettling phenomena. The whispers seemed to grow more coherent, forming chilling phrases and warnings. The shadows on the walls seemed to move independently, and the temperature fluctuations became more pronounced.

The family's fear reached new heights as the haunting continued to escalate. The malevolent presence within the house appeared to be growing stronger, and the disturbances became more frequent and intense.

The intensity of the haunting reached a new level when the witch's presence became more pronounced. The family experienced a series of terrifying encounters that seemed to be directly connected to the witch and her dark influence.

One night, John and Mary were awakened by a chilling sensation. The air in their bedroom was icy cold, and a low, guttural growl resonated through the room. The shadows on the walls seemed to stretch and twist, and the whispers grew louder.

The growling intensified, and a shadowy figure appeared in the corner of the room. The figure was vaguely human-shaped, with glowing eyes and an aura of malevolence. The figure moved closer, its presence exuding a palpable sense of dread.

John and Mary tried to confront the figure, but their attempts were met with a powerful, suffocating force. The shadows seemed to close in around them, and the whispers turned into a deafening roar. The figure's eyes glowed with an eerie light, and its presence was overwhelming.

Suddenly, the figure vanished, leaving the room in an unsettling silence. The temperature slowly returned to normal, but the sense of dread lingered. John and Mary were left shaken and exhausted, their fear deepening.

The witch's return was marked by a series of increasingly disturbing encounters. The family began to experience ghostly apparitions and nightmarish visions. The apparitions appeared to be trapped, their faces contorted in agony and despair.

The experiences were accompanied by a powerful, oppressive energy that seemed to suffocate the family. The shadows in the house grew darker and more menacing, and the whispers became a constant presence.

John and Mary realized that the witch's influence was more profound and pervasive than they had initially thought. The haunting had reached new heights of terror, and the family was faced with the daunting task of confronting the darkness that had taken hold of their home.

Desperate to find a solution, John and Mary turned to the occult books and documents they had discovered. They found a ritual described in one of the books that seemed to offer a potential way to bind the dark forces and neutralize their influence.

The ritual was known as the "Ritual of Binding," and it was designed to trap and contain malevolent entities. The ritual involved a series of complex steps, including the use of specific symbols, incantations, and protective items.

John and Mary gathered the necessary materials and prepared for the ritual. They set up the ritual space in the living room, placing the protective symbols and items around the room. They recited the incantations and performed the necessary steps, hoping that the ritual would help them confront and contain the dark forces.

As the ritual began, the house responded with increased intensity. The shadows on the walls seemed to writhe and twist, and the temperature dropped dramatically. The whispers grew louder, their voices blending into a chaotic cacophony.

The malevolent presence seemed to react to the ritual, its influence becoming more pronounced. The air grew thick with a suffocating energy, and the oppressive atmosphere intensified. The family struggled to maintain their focus as the ritual reached its climax.

The shadows in the room appeared to converge on the ritual space, and the oppressive energy became overwhelming. John and Mary continued to recite the incantations and perform the steps, their voices strained and desperate.

As the ritual neared its end, the malevolent presence seemed to resist the binding. The shadows grew darker, and the whispers turned into a deafening roar. The family's fear mounted as they faced the powerful, suffocating force.

The Ritual of Binding reached a critical point, and the malevolent presence within the house fought back with renewed ferocity. The shadows grew darker and more chaotic, and the oppressive energy became almost unbearable.

John and Mary struggled to complete the ritual, their fear and exhaustion taking a toll on their ability to focus. The whispers became a cacophony of voices, their words blending into an incomprehensible roar.

The malevolent presence seemed to resist the binding with all its power. The shadows writhed and twisted, and the temperature in the room plummeted. The family's sense of dread reached new heights as they faced the dark forces with unwavering determination.

In a final, desperate effort, John and Mary completed the last of the incantations and performed the final steps of the ritual. The shadows seemed to converge on the ritual space, and the oppressive energy began to dissipate.

As the ritual reached its conclusion, the room was filled with a blinding light. The shadows and whispers gradually faded, and the oppressive atmosphere began to lift. The family was left in an uneasy calm, their bodies trembling from the ordeal.

John and Mary were exhausted, their fear and anxiety palpable. The house felt different, but the sense of unease remained. They knew that their efforts had not fully resolved the haunting, and they remained vigilant in their efforts to understand and confront the darkness.

The Davis family faced an uncertain future. The haunting had reached new levels of terror, and the dark forces within their home seemed to be more resilient than they had anticipated. They continued to search for answers and solutions, hoping that their efforts would eventually bring them the peace and safety they so desperately sought.

CHAPTER 10: THE ECLIPSE OF TERROR

The aftermath of the Ritual of Binding had left the Davis family in a state of uneasy relief. The oppressive energy had lifted somewhat, but the house still exuded a sense of malevolence that refused to be ignored. Shadows continued to writhe on the walls, and the temperature fluctuations were erratic and unsettling.

John and Mary decided to take a brief respite from their investigations, hoping that some time away from the house would help them regain their strength. They took Lucy and Tom for a day trip to the nearby town, attempting to enjoy a moment of normalcy. However, the shadow of the house's dark presence lingered in their minds.

Upon returning, they found that the atmosphere in the house had changed. It felt heavier, as though the darkness had grown more insidious during their absence. The shadows seemed to pulse with a sinister rhythm, and the whispers that had receded were now more persistent and disconcerting.

That night, the family was plagued by a series of terrifying experiences. Lucy and Tom were once again haunted by nightmares, their dreams filled with grotesque figures and nightmarish scenarios. The nightmares were so vivid that the children woke up screaming, their faces contorted with fear.

John and Mary tried to comfort their children, but the nightmares continued to escalate. The children's fear began to affect their daily routines, and they became increasingly withdrawn and anxious. The once-cozy atmosphere of their home was now replaced by a pervasive sense of dread.

As the family struggled to cope with the disturbing experiences, they began to notice a series of eerie occurrences. The walls of the house seemed to whisper their fears, and the shadows took on more menacing shapes. The temperature fluctuations became more pronounced, and the air felt thick with an oppressive energy.

The house itself seemed to respond to the family's anxiety. The shadows on the walls grew darker and more chaotic, and the whispers became a constant presence. The oppressive atmosphere made it difficult for the family to find any sense of comfort or peace.

The haunting escalated as the malevolent presence within the house grew more aggressive. The Davis family experienced a series of horrifying encounters that seemed to defy explanation. The disturbances became more frequent and intense, and the darkness within the house seemed to take on a more tangible form.

One night, John and Mary were awakened by a series of loud, disorienting noises. The sounds came from various parts of the house—bangs, crashes, and the distinct sound of something scraping against the walls. The noises were accompanied by an overwhelming sense of dread.

John and Mary searched the house, trying to locate the source of the disturbances. They found nothing out of the ordinary, but the oppressive energy remained. The temperature continued to drop, and the whispers grew louder, their voices blending into a disorienting cacophony.

The disturbances extended to the children's rooms. Lucy and Tom reported hearing strange noises coming from their closets and under their beds. The noises were accompanied by a chilling sensation, as though something unseen was watching them.

John and Mary attempted to investigate, but their efforts were met with an unsettling silence. The shadows in the house seemed to move independently, and the air was thick with an oppressive energy. The family's fear grew as the unexplained occurrences continued.

One particularly terrifying night, the house was plunged into darkness. All the lights flickered and went out, leaving the family in an unsettling blackness. The whispers grew louder, and the shadows seemed to close in around them. The oppressive atmosphere made it difficult to breathe, and the family's fear reached new heights.

John and Mary tried to light candles and flashlights, but the darkness persisted. The shadows on the walls appeared to writhe and twist, and the whispers turned into a deafening roar. The family was left in a state of terror, unable to escape the overwhelming sense of dread.

Amidst the escalating terror, John and Mary decided to confront the witch directly. They hoped that a confrontation with the dark entity might offer some resolution to the haunting. They prepared to perform a ritual designed to reveal and banish the witch's presence.

The family gathered in the living room, setting up the ritual space with protective symbols and items. They recited the incantations and performed the necessary steps, hoping that their efforts would help them confront the malevolent force.

As they began the ritual, the house responded with increased intensity. The shadows on the walls grew darker and more chaotic, and the temperature dropped dramatically. The whispers became a cacophony of voices, their words blending into an incomprehensible roar.

The witch's presence became more pronounced as the ritual progressed. A shadowy figure began to materialize in the room, its eyes glowing with an eerie light. The figure moved closer, its malevolent energy suffusing the air.

John and Mary continued the ritual, their voices strained and desperate. They attempted to confront the witch, but their efforts were met with a powerful, suffocating force. The shadows seemed to close in around them, and the oppressive energy became almost unbearable.

The witch's form wavered and distorted, her presence exerting a powerful influence. The shadows writhed and twisted, and the whispers turned into a deafening roar. John and Mary struggled to maintain their focus as they faced the malevolent entity.

Suddenly, the witch's form dissolved into a swirling vortex of shadows. The oppressive energy gradually lifted, and the room was filled with a blinding light. The shadows and whispers faded, leaving the family in an uneasy calm.

Despite their best efforts, the Davis family's attempt to confront the witch had only intensified the haunting. The house seemed to be in the grip of a powerful, malevolent force that refused to be banished.

The days following the ritual were marked by a series of horrifying encounters. The shadows in the house grew darker and more chaotic, and the whispers became a constant presence. The temperature fluctuations became more extreme, and the oppressive atmosphere seemed to suffocate the family.

One night, the house was plunged into darkness once again. The lights flickered and went out, leaving the family in an unsettling blackness. The whispers grew louder, and the shadows on the walls seemed to close in around them.

The darkness was accompanied by a series of terrifying apparitions. The figures appeared to be trapped, their faces contorted in agony and despair. The apparitions moved through the house, their presence accompanied by an overwhelming sense of dread.

John and Mary attempted to confront the apparitions, but their efforts were met with an eerie silence. The shadows seemed to move independently, and the oppressive energy became almost unbearable. The family's fear reached new heights as they faced the dark forces that had taken hold of their home.

The eclipse of shadows seemed to mark a new phase in the haunting. The darkness within the house had become more tangible and malevolent, and the family was left to confront the terror that had taken over their lives.

Determined to find a solution, John and Mary decided to seek help from an expert in the occult. They reached out to a renowned paranormal investigator who had experience dealing with dark entities and malevolent forces.

The investigator arrived at the house and began conducting a thorough examination. They performed a series of tests and rituals to assess the nature of the dark forces and their influence on the house. The investigator's findings revealed that the malevolent presence was deeply rooted in the house's history.

The final confrontation was planned as a last-ditch effort to banish the dark forces and reclaim the home. The investigator, along with John and Mary, prepared to perform a powerful ritual designed to sever the connection between the house and the malevolent entities.

As the ritual began, the house responded with increased intensity. The shadows on the walls grew darker and more chaotic, and the whispers became a deafening roar. The oppressive energy in the room reached its zenith, and the family's fear was palpable.

The ritual was performed with precision and determination. The investigator led the ceremony, guiding John and Mary through the complex steps and incantations. The shadows seemed to converge on the ritual space, and the oppressive energy became almost unbearable.

As the ritual reached its climax, the malevolent presence began to waver. The shadows and whispers gradually faded, and the oppressive atmosphere lifted. The room was filled with a blinding light, and the darkness within the house seemed to dissipate.

The final confrontation marked a turning point in the haunting. The dark forces had been confronted and bound, and the oppressive energy that had pervaded the house began to lift. The Davis family faced an uncertain future, but the sense of dread and terror had been alleviated.

This chapter delves into the escalating terror faced by the Davis family, with the haunting reaching new heights of intensity and fear. It builds on the previous chapters, exploring the continued presence of the witch and the dark forces while introducing new elements and encounters. The chapter culminates in a dramatic final confrontation, offering a resolution to the terror that has plagued the family.

Chapter 11: The Relentless Haunting

The days that followed the final confrontation left the Davis family in a cautious state of relief. The heavy weight that seemed to envelop them had lifted somewhat, and the house was lighter. However, the uneasiness still lingered, and the darkness seemed merely to be lying in wait, awaiting its opportune time to strike.

The family tried to go back to some sort of normalcy, but

the haunting had left them with deep scars. John and Mary were always on edge, and the children, Lucy and Tom, were more withdrawn and anxious than ever. The once-cozy atmosphere of their home was replaced by an underlying tension that refused to dissipate.

One evening, the family was having dinner, and an chill seemed to fill the air. The temperature fell suddenly, and the room was filled with a sense of foreboding. The shadows on the walls seemed to grow darker, and the whispers that had receded returned with a vengeance.

Lucy and Tom started to feel scared, and their faces began to show the horror in their minds. John and Mary eyed each other with concern; this darkness was not fully eliminated. They tried to comfort their children, but fear was shown on their faces.

The disturbances grew more intense as they continued to eat: the shadows on the walls pulsed with a sinister rhythm, the whispers louder, more disorienting. The fluctuations in temperature are more pronounced, and the air seems to vibrate with oppressive energy.

In a second, the room plunged into darkness: lights flickered and went out, leaving the family in some sort of upsetting blackness. The whispers got louder, voices joining together in a deafening cacophony. It seemed like the shadows on the walls closed in around them, and the oppression became nearly unbearable.

The first thing John and Mary did was hasten to light candles and flashlights, getting rid of the darkness as much as possible. Flickering light danced on the walls, casting an eerie feeling in the atmosphere. The family sat together, their faces masks of growing terror.

The darkness seemed to take on a life of its own; the shadows twisted and writhed with malevolent intent. The whispers grew into chilling phrases, their words incomprehensible but full of menace. The family's fear reached new heights as they faced the unyielding darkness that had taken over their home.

With the continuous escalation of the haunting, their encounters with the supernatural became more frequent and intense. Apparitions that appeared during the eclipse of shadows now returned, and their presence was more pronounced, more terrifying.

One night, Lucy was awakened by a chilling sensation. She opened her eyes to see a shadowy figure standing at the foot of her bed. The figure was vaguely human-shaped, with glowing eyes and an aura of malevolence. Lucy's fear paralyzed her, and she could only watch in horror as the figure moved closer.

The face was twisted in a sort of agony, the eyes had a peculiar, malign light. A hand was stretched out toward Lucy, and an atmosphere of terror was about the figure. Lucy shrieked, her voice full of terror, and the figure went out, leaving her to shake and sob.

John and Mary rushed to their daughter's room, finding her in a state of hysterics. They tried to comfort her, but the fear in her eyes was unmistakable. The apparition's visit had left a deep mark on Lucy, and her fear only grew stronger.

Of course, Tom had also had his share of terrifying experiences. He says that he heard sounds in his closet and under his bed. There was a chilling sensation accompanying the noises-one like some unseen were watching him. One night, he saw a ghostly figure standing in the corner of his room, its eyes glowing with an eerie light.

The figure overwhelmed him, and a great feeling of dread overcame Tom. Tom attempted to call out for help, but terror had paralyzed his voice. The apparition drew closer, its malevolent energy suffusing the air. The fear reached a breaking point, and he screamed, causing the figure to vanish.

John and Mary were left to face the reality of their children's fear. The haunting reached new heights of terror, as if the malevolent presence in the house was reaching its peak. Their sense of safety lay shattered, and they were left right in front of the relentless darkness that had taken over their lives.

As the haunting continued, the malevolent entity within the house began to manifest more frequently. The family experienced a series of terrifying encounters that seemed to defy explanation. The darkness within the house took on a more tangible form, with disturbances intensifying.

In an instance, John and Mary were both awakened by disorienting sounds one night. The bangs, crashes, and the particular sound of scraping up the wall could be heard from different areas of the house. The feeling of dread that accompanied the noises was overwhelming.

They both explored every nook and corner of the house, trying to find out the source of this disturbance. Still, they found everything as normal, but the oppressive atmosphere in the house persisted. The temperature began falling as the whispering sounds turned louder-their voices becoming a cacophonous mess.

The events went as far as into the children's rooms; Lucy and Tom heard funny noises in their closets and beneath their beds. There was a chilling feeling with the noises, some unseeable object still watching them. John and Mary tried to investigate, but all efforts led to an unsettling silence.

With that, the malevolent entity seemed to grow more aggressive, its presence more pronounced. One of those really terrible nights, house occupants were plunged again into darkness, lights flickering and heaving until they just went out, leaving them in some really unsettling blackness. The whispers grew louder, and the shadows on the walls seemed to close in around them.

With the darkness came a succession of ghostly apparitions: figures which seemed to be trapped, contorted in agony and despair. The apparitions moved through the house, accompanied by an overwhelming sense of dread.

Confronting the apparitions, John and Mary tried in all ways to speak with them, but the only answer was that macabre silence. The shadows moved by themselves, and the feeling of suffocation there was almost unbearable. The fear among the family members reached a new height, as they faced the dark forces that had taken hold of their home.

The malevolent entity was fully overwhelming, and the family did not know how to cope with the terror that kept growing. It seemed as though the darkness in the house was closing in around them, and the sense of dread was palpable. The fear and anxiety of the family reached a breaking point as they faced the relentless haunting that had taken over their lives.

The haunting intensified; the presence of the witch intensified. A host of terrifying experiences began to plague the family seemingly linked directly with the witch and her dark influence. The disturbances grew stronger and the malevolent energy within the house almost became unbearable.

One night, John and Mary were awakened by a chilling sensation. The air in their bedroom was icy cold, and a low, guttural growl resonated through the room. The shadows on the walls seemed to stretch and twist, and the whispers grew louder.

The growling became louder, and in the corner of the room, a figure materialized out of the darkness. It took on roughly a human form but was indistinct except for its glowing eyes and aura of malevolence. The figure moved closer, its presence thick with dread.

John and Mary tried to face up to the figure, but their efforts were met by a powerful suffocating force. The shadows seemed to close in around them, and the whispers turned into a deafening roar. His eyes glowed with an otherworldly light, and his presence was overwhelming.

Then, in an instant, it was gone, leaving the room silent, eerily so. The temperature would eventually stabilize, but the feeling of dread lingered. John and Mary were shaking and exhausted with their fear much deeper now.

The witch's grip tightened on the family, and her powers were growing stronger day by day. The haunting had reached new heights of terror, and it was time for the family to take the challenge of standing up against the darkness that had grasped their home.

The continuous persecution from the haunter wore down their psyche, causing a mental deterioration in the mind and emotions of the Davis family. Having been made to live in constant fear and anxiety, their grip with reality slowly deteriorated, while they were simultaneously spiraling into insanity.

John and Mary grew paranoid amid all the fear and anxiety. They can hardly differentiate realities from supernatural forces, and slowly, their marriage began to get strained due to continuous pressure.

The haunting also greatly affected Lucy and Tom, who

started having more frequent and vivid nightmares and could not find any comfort or sense of safety. The children became even more fearful and anxious, turning inward and isolating themselves.

A series of surreal and disturbing confrontations marked their spiral into lunacy. Shadows on the wall began to appear more grotesque, and the whispered voices were constantly present. Almost unbearable was this heavy atmosphere in the house, a feeling of paranoia at its very height.

The Davis family was thrown into a very uncertain future; their lives were consumed by the haunting. The malevolent presence in their home would not let up, and the family's sense of safety and sanity was in tatters. They were left to face the darkness that had taken over their lives, their fear and determination their only allies in the battle against the supernatural forces that plagued them.

It was in the midst of this spiral into madness that the Davis family learned more about the tragic events that had contributed to the house's dark history. Determined to understand the malevolent forces in full measure, John and Mary explored the most hidden parts of the mansion in search of clues that might lead them to put an end to the haunting.

First, they went to the attic, where the chest was kept which Mary had found earlier along with the Ouija boards, books on witchcraft, and spells. This time, they thoroughly rummaged through them and found lots of confusing notes and some diaries depicting dark rituals, a witch's deal with forces of darkness.

But one diary stood out for Mary. It was from their uncle,

now deceased, and described his decline into the dark arts. He wrote of meetings with the witch-a powerful, vengeful spirit that required blood sacrifices to maintain her grasp on the mansion.

An old blueprint of the house that John found revealed a hidden room in the basement. With growing trepidation, they decided to investigate. The basement was already a place of deep unease for the family, its dark corners and cold stone walls filled with an oppressive sense of dread.

They had found it behind a huge, decaying cabinet; heavy, it creaked ominously while they pried it open. Inside, they came upon a small, dimly lit chamber with occult symbols painted on the walls. The air was thick with the stench of decay, and some kind of dark energy pulsed from every surface.

In the center of the room, there was an altar, tarnished with what appeared to be old blood. Surrounding it were sundry artifacts: animal bones, strange substances in jars, and a very ancient book bound in human skin. It contained arcane symbols and spells, many identical to those in the chest that Mary had found.

As they looked around the room, the temperature abruptly dropped, and the whispers grew louder, their words melting into a maddening chorus of menace. The shadows on the wall appeared to be moving of their own accord; the feeling of being watched overwhelmed them.

Suddenly, a cold wind whipped through the room and doused their flashlight. They heard a low, guttural growl that seemed to emanate from the walls themselves. The malevolent presence was stronger here; it was as if the room served as a focal point for the dark energy that pervaded the house.

They hastened to leave the chamber, shut the door firmly

behind them, and rushed on. They had found the missing piece of the puzzle, but they also understood that a head-on attack by the malevolent forces could not be done merely by knowledge.

The finding of the hidden chamber only escalated the terror. The presence in the house became even more aggressive, while torments from the witch became more personal and violent. Each family member faced harrowing encounters that left them shaken and fearful.

She began to see the witch more often. The apparition would appear at random moments, her face twisted in rage and sorrow. One evening, as Lucy was doing her homework, she looked up to find the witch standing by her window, staring in with eyes glowing with malevolence. Lucy screamed and the figure disappeared, but the fear did not.

Equally terrifying were Tom's experiences. One night, he felt something crawling over his skin, and he woke up to see shadowy hands emerging from beneath his bed, touching him with icy coldness. He tried to scream, but his voice was caught in his throat. The hands disappeared just as suddenly as they appeared, leaving him paralyzed with fear.

Nor did John and Mary escape from the torture of the witch. Quite often, John would wake up at midnight and was unable to move; the witch's face would be inches away from his face. Her breath was cold, reeking of decaying substances, and her whispered words would echo in his head with thoughts of despair and futility.

For her part, Mary started to hear the witch's voice during the day. It was first sweetly whispered and then building into more strident cries, she heard nothing else. The voice was telling her terrible things about the house and some pact that was made by her uncle.

One very frightening night, Mary again saw the witch hanging from the tree outside the attic window. This time, she distinctly heard the voice of the witch whispering uttering some sort of curses and threats. Mary ran downstairs and out of the house, but it was gone. The earth below the tree was not disturbed, as if the witch had never been there.

The experiences of the family were driving them to the brink of madness. They were exhausted and always on edge, their fear and anxiety consuming their every thought. The malevolent forces inside the house seemed to be getting stronger, feeding off their terror.

The haunting had finally gotten to their nerves and minds continuously. Desperate for answers, desperate for a way to end the terror that had taken over their lives, John called the paranormal investigator who helped them before in search of a solution.

The investigator arrived with a team of experts dealing with dark entities and supernatural forces. They thoroughly searched the house, fitted with the latest equipment to scan and measure paranormal activity.

What they found was disturbing: the house was a focal point of dark energy, anchored by the rituals conducted by John's uncle and the malevolent presence of the witch. It was discovered that this hidden chamber in the basement was the source of the dark energy-a portal for malevolent entities.

The investigator explained that the spirit of the witch was bound to the house by a very powerful curse. To break the curse, a very elaborate and dangerous ritual would be required-one that could perhaps banish the witch and the dark entities forever. However, it would also put the family in great danger, for the malevolent forces would surely fight back with all their might.

They decided to follow through with the ritual despite such danger. They did not want to live in fear for the rest of their lives anymore, and they prepared themselves for some kind of nightmare that would save their family.

The preparation for the ritual was very intense, a bit beyond their nerves. The investigator and his team had set up protective wards and symbols throughout the house to create a barrier to contain the dark energy. The steps of the ritual were taught to the family, and the importance of them being focused and as one was reiterated.

It was to be performed within the hidden chamber, the heart of the house's dark energy. The family was pale and tense as they congregated in the basement. The investigator led the ceremony, guiding them through the incantations and rituals needed to break the curse.

It was not until the ritual finally got underway that the house reacted with greater vigour: darker and wilder shadows on the walls, whispers growing into a deafening roar, drastically falling temperatures, and oppressive energy that was almost unbearable.

The forces of evil retaliated, and the dark, twisted figures of evil seemed to materialize from the shadows. The figures moved closer toward the family, their eyes aglow with malevolence. The protective wards held them at bay, but the pressure was immense.

Hand in hand, John and Mary's voices were firm and unwavering, though each was terrified with fear. Standing close to each other, Lucy and Tom seemed set upon a determination to get the haunting over with. And then the incantations continued-a rumbling of voice from the whole family. The witch's presence strengthened with the advancement of the ritual. She started to take form in the middle of the room, her eyes full of anger and sadness. She began walk-

ing towards the family, bathing them in her evil aura.
The investigator continued to lead the ritual, his voice strong and unwavering. The family's fear was palpable, but their determination was stronger. They recited the final incantation, calling upon the powers of light to banish the darkness.
A blinding light filled the room, and the malevolent entities screamed in agony. The witch's form wavered and distorted, her presence dissolving into the light. The oppressive energy was lifted, and the shadows on the walls faded. And then the room was filled with an overwhelming sense of peace and relief.
The ritual of banishment marked the close of the haunting. For the first time, the dark forces that had tormented the Davis family were vanquished, and a sense of peace and tranquility filled the house. The oppressive energy was gone, replaced by a warm, comforting presence.
The family was tired but relieved. The terror and anxiety that filled their life slowly vanished, and they started to build their life anew. But the memories of the haunting stayed with them, a fact that, at last, they had stood against dark forces and had triumphed over it.
The investigator and his team reassured the family that the curse was now broken, and the malevolent forces would not return. They left the family with protective charms and rituals to maintain the peace and ensure the house remained free from dark influences.
And so, John, Mary, Lucy, and Tom slowly healed from their ordeal. They regained their home and filled it with light and love. The rooms that were once dreaded became comforting, while the shadows that once haunted them were now memories.
The Davis family had been battered by unconscionable ter-

ror, yet through it all, they emerged in one piece: stronger, firmer, and united. Both knew the happenings irrevocably changed them, but that gave them an altogether new appreciation of how strong love and determination could be. Overcome was the darkness, and finally, the family could see a future with no fear.

Chapter 12: Relentless Terror

The peace following the ritual of banishment was short-lived. Despite the apparent success in vanquishing the malevolent forces, the Davis family soon found themselves plunged back into a world of terror and fear. The darkness they had believed to have been expelled began to seep back into their lives, more insidious and pervasive than before.

It was John who first picked up portents. He woke in the middle of the night to a soft, dissonant music apparently seeping from some quarter of the house. He thought it an artifact of his imagination, but the music got louder and more distinct. It was an eerie melody in the air-an eldritch tune that seemed to tug at his very soul.

Out of the bed and down the hall, he followed the sound to the living room. There, in the poor light, was the figure, sitting at the old piano which came with the house. Its back was to him, but something cold and evil emanated from it. As he entered, the figure turned, showing him the gaunt, hollow-eyed face of the witch. A wicked smile contorted her mouth, and she vanished, leaving John to shudder and wonder about his sanity.

The morning after, John tried to tell Mary about the encounter as she, in turn, was already on edge from what happened to her. She woke up in the middle of the night to see her reflection staring at her with pure hatred in her eyes from the bathroom mirror. It moved of its own accord, its eyes aglow with an evil light, before it exploded into a thousand pieces. The children came running at Mary's scream, but when they arrived, there was no broken glass to be seen.

Lucy and Tom did not get away scot-free either. Lucy began to hear the whispering voices again, this time from her closet. The voices whispered in some ancient, guttural language, instilling in her a deep sense of foreboding. She could feel cold hands brushing against her skin, and at night, she saw shadowy figures lurking at the edge of her vision.

Tom's experiences were not any less hair-raising. Periodically, he woke up with scratch marks and bruises which he couldn't explain. One evening, he felt himself being pinned down in his bed, unable to move. Cold breath fanned across his face, and the witch's chilling laughter seemed to ring in his ears. When he broke loose, claw marks dug into the headboard of his bed were a vivid reality.

The attempts of the family to seek his help were drowned out in dead silence. No phone calls, no e-mails; it was as if the ghost hunter and his crew had vanished into thin air. Then desperation kicked in, and the Davis family knew they were left to face this unyielding terror, again come upon their home.

The haunting grew in strength and the house became a battleground between the living and the dead. The veil separating the physical world from the supernatural was wearing thin; malevolent entities could cross over with much more ease than before. The family's reality became a nightmarish blend of distorted visions and horrifying encounters.

One night, John and Mary were hanging around the kitchen when, all of a sudden, the room got cold. The lights started to blink and went dead, putting them in complete dark.

The heavy silence was disrupted only by the clear footsteps, which were very slow and heavy, echoing through the house. The footsteps sounded louder, accompanied with whispers reaching from every side in a chorus.

John took a flashlight and lit it around the room; there was nothing. The footsteps continued, and the air grew colder. Mary clutched John's arm, her fear palpable. They heard a low growl, and a shadowy figure appeared in the doorway, its eyes glowing with an eerie light. The figure moved toward them, and they could feel its malevolent energy suffusing the air.

It vanished just as it appeared, with John and Mary in states of horror and shock. They knew full well that the house was under siege from forces beyond their comprehension, and the tenuous membrane between worlds enabled the malevolent entities to impress their will upon them more strongly than before.

No less harrowing was it for Lucy and Tom either. First, Lucy started having this awful dream in which some incomprehensible dark silhouettes were after her through twisted corridors of some sort, having a house somehow in it, calling out her name, whispering menacingly. Getting up from sleep, she found the feeling of the dreams clung on to her long after she opened her eyes-messy and scared. The basement also beckoned him with an undeniable attraction, something that he abhorred. One night, he had an irresistible urge to go down the stairs, and his feet were moving of their own accord. The basement was pitch black, and a feeling of foreboding weighed heavily in the air. It was at the bottom step that he saw the creaking open of the door to the hidden chamber, showing him the altar and the dark symbols painted on the walls. A chill, malevolent presence permeated the room, and Tom felt a hand grip his shoulder. He whirled, but no one was there. He ran back upstairs, his heart pounding in his chest.

The events in the family began to increase in frequency and to become scarier: things moved around by themselves, and doors would shut without any apparent reason, while whispers grew louder and more insistent. The house throbbed as if with life-a life fed by dark energy, breaking down the edges between the everyday and otherworldly.

Overwhelmed, John and Mary felt themselves taking another move. They determined that they themselves were going to research back into the history of the house, hoping eventually to find the way to chase malevolent forces completely from their premises. Hours were used poring through old records, documents, trying to piece together the dark, strong legacy and the influence of this mansion and that witch.

Further research revealed that a series of unexplained deaths and disappearances had taken place regarding the house throughout the years, each incident in relation to the rituals conducted in the chamber, and how the spirit of the witch was confined within the house by a very powerful curse. They also found mentions of a very powerful cleansing ritual which might actually break the curse and banish dark entities once and for all.

With the knowledge compiled, John and Mary prepared to face off for the last time against the forces of evil. They were aware that this cleansing ritual was going to be dangerous; they, however, would not be turned back in setting things right with this haunting. Thus, they obtained ingredients and ritual tools necessary, including charms and symbols of protection, and prepared the stage in the hidden chamber.

That night of the ritual, the house was heavy with repressive silence. The family gathered in the basement, faces pale and strained. The air was thick with the foreboding feeling, and the shadows danced around them as if they were alive.

John and Mary led the incantations-ritual clear, though their hearts jellified in fear. Lifting their voices in unison to the powers of light, banishing the forces of darkness that attacked them, they continued to say the incantations they had found. It slowly grew colder, and this force of oppression seemed almost insupportable; the shadows danced tortured on walls, and the whispered tone louder, their voice tones blending together to a deafening roar.

At this stage of the development, the baneful forces started fighting back with all their might. The grotesque figures emerged from the dark; their eyes were glowing with malevolence. The family moved in their direction, emitting a palpable sense of dread.

Undaunted, John and Mary clasped hands. Lucy and Tom stood close by, their faces masks of fear and determination. In unison, the family spoke the final incantation, their voices rising in one mighty crescendo.

A blinding brilliance enveloped the room, and the devilish creatures shrieked in anguished appeals. The witch's body materialized center room, the eyes afire with anger and sadness. Approaching the family, her malevolent spirit filled the room.

The light grew brighter and brighter, with the witch's form starting to waver and distort. The oppressive energy lifted, and the shadows on the walls began to fade. The room was filled with an overwhelming sense of peace and relief as the witch's presence dissolved into the light.

The family stood in stunned silence, their terror slowly giving way to a sense of triumph. For the first time, the dark forces that had plagued their lives were finally vanquished, and the house was filled with tranquility and peace.

The cleansing ritual marked the end of the haunting. Gone was the oppressive energy that had filled the house, replaced by a warm, comforting presence. The family was exhausted but relieved; finally, their fear and anxiety gave way to a sense of peace.

John, Mary, Lucy, and Tom began the long process of rebuilding their lives, reclaiming their home, and filling it with light and love. The memories of the haunting lingered, but the knowledge that they had faced and overcome the darkness gave them strength. The shadows that had once haunted them were now just memories, and the house became a place of comfort and safety once again.

These were unimaginable terrors the Davis family had to go through and come out even stronger and united. They both knew how their experience had changed them, but it rather allowed them to appreciate the power of love and determination. Overcame was the darkness, and at long last, the family was able to look with hope toward a future not dictated by fear.

They kept the protective charms and symbols so that the house would remain a place of light. The veil between the worlds had been mended, and the evil beings were gone once and for all. They felt peace again in their hearts because they knew it: they overcame the persistent terror and won their lives back.

The Davis family cherished every moment spent together now, and the bonding had become stronger than ever. Having faced the darkness and emerging victorious, this love and resilience stood tall to test their strength. The house was no longer the house of fear and dread but the symbol of the triumph of themselves over the supernatural forces that were after them to destroy them.

Going ahead in the future with lots of hope, the Davis family still held inside the scars on and forever would act like a reminder for them all for the days in darkness that prevailed earlier. While this haunting apparently subsided, some or other hints reverberated continuous echoes within their house regarding what happened. They would sometimes catch glimpses of the supernatural: shadows that would seem to move of their own accord, cold spots in rooms, and very late at night, the faint sound of dissonant music. Minor incidents compared to the terror they had faced, yet a reminder that some of the history of the mansion would never be eradicated.

One afternoon, while in the attic, Lucy found an old photo album, which was hidden in a trunk covered with dust. The photos documented the history of the mansion, from its construction to the different families that had lived there over the decades. Among them, one really called her interest: a photo of people standing in front of the house, faces all somber and eyes hollow. Among them was the witch, her presence unmistakable even in the faded image.

She showed the album to her parents, and they pieced together more of the mansion's history. They learned that the witch, once a respected healer in the community, had been wrongfully accused of witchcraft by jealous townspeople. Her execution had been a tragic and unjust event, and her spirit had lingered, seeking vengeance against those who had wronged her and anyone who dared to live in her home.

This new comprehension of the sad story of the witch awakened a kind of sympathy in the family. In a way, the witch had been a victim, just as they were. This was the realization that John and Mary came to when considering their actions to secure their home in peace.

A plan had been made in order to bring the tormented spirit of a witch to a peaceful close: the help of a local historian and the involvement of spiritual media. Settle her spirit-the Davis family did-thoughts on the way that might finally honor the witch's memory and make amends for her suffering.

He gave them a detailed account of the life of the witch: the service she had given to the community as a healer, the circumstances that brought her to such a sad end. The medium, in turn, proposed a rite of remembrance, which would give public recognition to the memory of the witch and a formal apology for the wrongs she suffered.

They decided to have it in the garden of the mansion, right next to the tree on which the witch was hanged. They invited the medium and the historian and a few close friends who stood by them through their ordeal. They erected a shrine together-adorned with flowers and candles-with a plaque to commemorate the life of the witch and the wrongs that were done to her.

As the sun began to set, the medium led the ceremony; she called for peace and reconciliation. She talked about the witch's contribution to the community and the injustice of her execution. The family and their friends each took turns to say their sorries and appreciation for the witch's life.

As the ceremony reached its climax, a warm, gentle breeze swept through the garden, and the oppressive energy that had once suffused the mansion seemed to lift completely. The family felt a profound sense of peace, as if a long-standing wound had finally begun to heal.

It was only now, when the spirit of the witch had been laid to rest, that the Davis family was free from the haunting. The mansion had turned into a haven filled with light and love where the echoes of the past did not hold them back. Shadows haunting their lives would be mere memory.

The witch's memory continued to be respected by the family, who kept her shrine in the garden, occasionally holding minor ceremonies in her memory. This was a comforting act of remembrance, fortifying the bond shared and lessons learnt.

John and Mary devoted themselves to rebuilding their lives, giving Lucy and Tom a stable and loving environment. The children slowly felt secure again, and their nightmares grew fewer and fewer until they stopped. The family started inviting friends and neighbors over, filling the mansion with laughter and joy.

The experience had changed them all; it had made them more resilient, more together. They had faced unimaginable terror and emerged stronger, their love and determination overcoming the darkness that once sought to consume them.

Years went by, and the mansion started to become a cherished home, while its dark history was smothered by the love and happiness the Davis family had filled its halls with. The neighborhood, once fearing the old mansion, began to recognize it as the symbol of strength and renewal.

In time, the tale of the Davis family treading a path from fear and darkness into peace and light flowered into local legend-a testament to the power of love, resilience, and understanding and compassion. The mansion now stood proud as a beacon of hope, a reminder that even in the darkest places, the light of love and unity could transform the setting.

In the end, the Davis family found not just a house but a true home: one where the past was acknowledged and respected, and the future was filled with promise and joy.

Their story became a part of the mansion's legacy, a new chapter that spoke of triumph over adversity and the enduring strength of the human spirit.

Chapter 13: The Unveiling of Hidden Horrors

The Davis family had finally gotten their lives back to as normal as it could be, considering what they had gone through with the supernatural. But as summer approached and the days became longer, John felt it was time to attend to some long-overdue home improvements. Among them was to finally explore the basement and renovate it, which had been largely left untouched since the initial cleansing ritual.

John started the exploration one Saturday afternoon, armed with a flashlight and a toolkit. The basement was huge, its walls lined with old shelves full of forgotten relics and boxes full of dust. He worked his way through the clutter, determined to make the space usable.

As John cleaned part of the basement, he noticed that something didn't quite fit. One wall just didn't match the others. The bricks were newer and less worn; even the pattern was somewhat different. Curious, he tapped on the wall, and the wall returned a hollow echo. Now that his curiosity was aroused, John had to investigate further.

He pulled out a hammer and chisel from his toolbox and started chiseling the bricks out with care. As he worked, an uneasy feeling settled over him, but he pushed it aside, focused on uncovering whatever lay behind the wall. After several hours of painstaking labour, he succeeded in making an opening large enough to look through.

A musty, stale smell wafted from the darkness, and John shone his flashlight inside. The beam revealed a hidden chamber, much like the one they had found earlier in their ordeal. This room, however, was different. It was larger and filled with strange, unsettling artifacts: old, rotting furniture, faded tapestries with grotesque imagery, and shelves lined with jars containing unidentifiable substances.

As John stepped through the opening, he felt a cold draft, and the hairs on the back of his neck stood up. It was as if the room was pulsating with some sort of malevolent energy, as if something dark and ancient had been locked in for centuries. He went farther inside, despite his feelings of growing trepidation, the flashing of his flashlight ominously dancing across his feet.

He walked down to the other end of the room and came across a very big, baroque mirror that was completely covered in thick dust. He wiped it off, and there was a sudden, strong pressure inside the room as if the air pressed against him with weight. He saw his reflection in the mirror, but it was wrong somehow: his eyes looked hollow, and his face was twisted in a cruel grin.

John had recoiled in horror and turned, knocking over a shelf in his hastened retreat. The resounding noise from the chamber was deafening, and turning to leave, he noticed something even more disturbing: a dark form standing in the corner of the room, hardly distinguishable in the faint light, appeared to be regarding him, a tangible presence of evil.

Panicking, John ran from the hidden chamber and back into the main basement. He quickly bricked up the wall again, hoping to seal whatever he had unleashed back inside. But as he did, he couldn't shake the feeling that it was already too late—that something had escaped, something far more dangerous than anything they had faced before.

That night, the Davis family began to experience a new wave of disturbances. It started subtly at first-doors opening and closing on their own, objects disappearing and reappearing in odd places, and strange, unidentifiable noises echoing through the halls. These occurrences quickly escalated, becoming more aggressive and terrifying.

Mary was the first to encounter the new entity directly. She had been in the kitchen, preparing dinner, when one of the cabinet doors, with a great deal of force, slammed shut and broke all the glasses inside. Startled, she turned to see a chair slide across the floor, as if an invisible hand had pushed it. The air grew cold, and she could hear a faint whispering, though nothing could be clearly deciphered. Terrified, she called out for John, who came in to find her pale and trembling.

John reassured her, but inwardly he knew this new haunting had something to do with his basement discovery. He didn't want to worry the children, so he kept such suspicions to himself for the time being.

Not even Lucy and Tom could escape the poltergeist's wrath. One evening, while Lucy was doing her homework in her room, her desk started shaking violently. Books flew off the shelves, and her lamp flickered erratically. She screamed for her parents, but by the time they arrived, everything had returned to normal. Lucy was left in tears, her fear and confusion evident.

Equally harrowing were Tom's experiences. He woke up in the middle of the night to find his bed shaking or his toys in menacing formations. One night, he woke to feel something cold and clammy clutching his ankle and tugging him towards the edge of the bed. He managed to break free and ran into his parents' room, his face white with terror.

The family tried to put up with the growing disturbances, but it soon became apparent that this new entity was a great deal more powerful and malevolent than those previous spirits with which they had already dealt. The activities of the poltergeist grew more violent, its presence seeming to pervade every corner of the house.

Soon enough, John and Mary realized that they were in over their heads. They called the historian and the medium who had helped them before, in the hope that one of them might have an inkling about this new danger. Upon hearing what had happened, the historian became deeply concerned; he informed them that most hidden chambers-like the one John opened-are utilized for dark rituals, and the act of opening them may result in powerful and malevolent entities being freed.

The medium, upon arriving at the house, immediately sensed the presence of the poltergeist and another, even darker entity. She did a cleansing ritual, but it had little effect. The poltergeist's activities continued unabated, and the shadowy figure John had seen in the hidden chamber began to appear more frequently.

The shadowy figure now became known as the Shadow Man, and he was in the Davis household to stay. Unlike the poltergeist, which seemed to revel in the mayhem and terror it could elicit, the Shadow Man projected an aura of cold, calculated evil. He would appear in the corners of rooms, watching silently with his glowing red eyes, his form shifting and flickering like a dark flame.

One night, John saw the Shadow Man when he went into Tom's room to check on him because he had been having nightmares. As he came into the room, he saw the Shadow Man standing at the foot of the bed, staring at his son. John felt a surge of protective rage and yelled at the entity to leave his family alone. The Shadow Man simply stared at him before dissolving into darkness, leaving John in a helpless and terrified state.

Equally disturbing were Mary's encounters with the Shadow Man: the way he appeared behind her in the mirrors, looming over her with those piercing red eyes. She could feel his cold presence in the room-a chill that seemed to seep right into her bones. The fear and anxiety took a toll on her, and she started losing sleep, constantly on edge, waiting for the next appearance.

But Lucy and Tom were terrorized by him, too. She would dream about him, standing at the foot of her bed or lurking in the dark corners of her room. Tom was already traumatized by the poltergeist's antics; now he had to deal with the silent, looming menace of the Shadow Man. The palpable fear and despair began to fray family cohesion.

Yet, the medium and the historian did everything in their power, but they could not rid them of the Shadow Man. The medium explained that the Shadow Man was probably an embodiment of pure evil lured into the house by the dark energy released from the hidden chamber. She said, maybe they have to perform some stronger ritual to banish him, but such a ritual would be dangerous and require great preparation.

He felt so guilty for having released this new terror upon his family and was determined to find a solution. He continued researching the history of the mansion, learning more about the dark rituals that had been conducted there. He found that the original owner of the mansion, a man named Elias Blackwood, had practiced dark magic; Blackwood had conducted many rituals in the hidden chamber in his pursuit of power and immortality. It was surmised that one of these rituals had bound the Shadow Man to the house.

With the historian guiding them, John and Mary prepared

for the final confrontation against the Shadow Man and the poltergeist. They gathered all the items needed for the ritual, including rare herbs, protective symbols, and a powerful cleansing incantation. The medium gave them a detailed plan wherein they were supposed to lure the entities into the hidden chamber and trap them there before the banishing ritual could be performed.

The night of the ritual, the air was thick with foreboding. Pale but resolute, the family sat in the basement as the medium began the ritual, chanting in some language that seemed to reverberate through the walls of the mansion itself. The air turned cold, and the lights began to flicker as the poltergeist and the Shadow Man materialized.

The poltergeist lashed out-objects flying, walls shaking-but the family held their ground. The medium's chants grew louder and louder, and then the Shadow Man appeared; his eyes, red with rage, were ablaze. He moved closer to them, his presence cold and suffocating.

Still hand in hand, John and Mary boldly faced the Shadow Man and said the banishing incantation that the medium taught them. And then the loud roared which echoed within this mansion was his roar, and not being able to press closer-the medium gave to the ritual the last drops of strength and directed these beings at the hidden chamber. She then instructed John to shut the wall up anew while all were pulled into this chamber. Now shaking all over, John proceeded to brick the entrance up anew as the poltergeist and Shadow Man fought the tugging of the ritual. Air thickened momentously while all sounds of scuffles filled the room.

The ritual was over when the medium replaced the last brick. With a shiny flash, there burst a vivid light into the dark basement, and it really looked as though that oppressive sensation hovering over this house started to go away. That had worn down the family once and for all.

The quiet and peaceful mansion was different now. The lingering sense of malevolence was gone, replaced by a calm, soothing energy. The Davis family had been through unimaginable horrors, but they had emerged victorious, their bond stronger than ever.

In the following weeks, the Davis family tried to put their lives together. The mansion, which had once terrorized and been dark, became the will and strength of their existence. The secret chamber was shut down, wordlessly, silently telling of the horrors they had encountered and were able to survive.

Grateful that their family was safe, John and Mary channeled all their energy into providing a warm and loving environment for Lucy and Tom. The children, though still recovering from the trauma they experienced, started to feel secure and happy once again.

And then, the community, upon hearing about their family's bravery and determination, gave them support and friendship. The mansion, now freed from its dark past, would become a beacon of light and love, the testament of unity and resilience.

The Davis family had come out of the most terrifying ride of fear and darkness, yet were more solid than ever, and the bonding tighter. Their story became a part of the mansion's legacy: a new chapter added to its annals, which spoke about victory over misfortune and unbreakable human spirits.

Eventually, the Davis family came to find, instead of just a house, a real home where the past was acknowledged and respected, while the future shone bright with promise and joy. Their story became a part of the mansion's legacy-a testament to the power of love, resilience, and the importance of understanding and compassion.

Chapter 14: Return of the Witch The nightmare of living with a poltergeist and a Shadow Man had slowly come to an end for the Davis family. Their home, which once knew no comfort from dread and despair, had started becoming a light-and-warm-filled place again. Well, all that was just to last a short time.

One evening, while cleaning the study, John had found an ancient leather-bound book hidden behind one row of dusty books. Curious, he had flipped through its pages. The journal apparenlty belonged to Elias Blackwood-the original owner of this mansion and, reputedly a dark sorcerer, the source behind all this hauntful stir that happens within its walls.

John was fascinated and appalled by Blackwood's accounts in minute detail about his rituals and experiments. Among these, he chanced upon one entry that particularly grabbed his attention-that of a rather powerful summoning ritual, intended to bind the spirit of a witch accused healer unto the mansion, to a bond of servitude. The witch's name was Eleanor, and, according to Blackwood, it was she from whom much of the dark energy had emanated around the mansion.

The journal also referred to an unfinished spell, one that Blackwood had planned to use in order to full and complete control over Eleanor's spirit but had never finished. It was as if, while reading the last lines in the journal, John felt a cold shiver run down his spine. It seemed the spirit of the witch was not at rest, and recent disturbances might have been the result of her growing strength.

Determined to protect his family, John decided to share his discovery with Mary and the medium that had helped them before. This night, in the living room where the family was congregated, John showed them the contents of the journal. Mary paled while the children listened with wide, fearful eyes.

The medium, after having looked at the journal, confirmed John's worst fears. Eleanor's spirit had been partially freed by the rituals earlier in the year, but Blackwood's unfinished spell had left her trapped and angry. She probably caused the recent disturbances in attempts to communicate and seek vengeance.

The medium proposed a new ritual that would either finally free Eleanor's spirit or send her away from the mansion forever. She warned them that the ritual would be dangerous and required careful preparation. The family, though terrified, agreed that they had no choice but to confront the witch once more.

Days blended together as the family began their frantic preparation for the ritual. The rare herbs, candles, and all sorts of talismans of protection were all they were gathering. All the steps to take were explained by the medium, underlining above all the importance of being united and concentrated.

As the night of the ritual approached, tension mounted inside the mansion. Peculiar things began to happen more frequently, with a surge in violence: doors slamming, rattling of windows, and flying objects around the room. The temperature dropped while the air seemed to crackle with some unseen energy.

It was in the living room of the house that the ritual took place-the family gathered on the night it was to happen. Following the medium's instructions, they prepared an altar and the medium initiated the proceedings in her low, melodic voice that seemed to take on a resonating tone with the very walls of the mansion.

As the ritual went on, the temperature in the room began to freeze, and an eerie silence fell. The medium continued her chanting, and the candles flickered, casting long dancing shadows on the walls. Then, a cold wind blew through the room, extinguishing the candles and sending the room into darkness.

In the poor light, the family saw her-the witch, Eleanor, standing at the edge of the room. Her eyes shone with an otherworldly light, and her presence exuded a palpable sense of anger and sorrow. She began to speak, her voice echoing as if coming from a great distance.

You dare to summon me?" she spat, her gaze riveted upon John. "You who have disturbed my rest, who have opened the door to darkness?"

John, his voice quivering, came forward. "We want to put this to an end, Eleanor. We would like to free you from all this pain.

Eleanor's face relaxed a trifle, her anger still in her voice: "You cannot undo what has been done. Blackwood's curse binds me here, and your actions have only strengthened it."

The medium, sensing urgency, resumed chanting-ancient spirits of protection to assist in the ritual. Energy swirled thick in the air, the candles re-igniting themselves and burning brighter than before.

Eleanor shrieked with frustration, her figure blurring and writhing about. The family stood firm, their eyes on the medium's repetitions and the protection circle they had formed. Gradually, the anger of the witch began to subside, replaced by an intense, sad resignation.

Conclusively, he invoked the spirits of light to help in liberating Eleanor from this earthbound state. There was an awfully brilliant light that pervaded the space; Eleanor's body became less and less dense, while on her face, it wore pain and longing.

By this time, John was steady as he spoke direct to Eleanor. "We can understand your pain, know the bad things that have been done to you, want to help you find rest.
Her eyes met his, and in that moment, all anger, all sorrow seemed to dissipate. "Peace," she whispered. "I have not known peace for so long.
The chant of the medium grew louder, the protective circle radiant with light. Eleanor's form began to break down, her features softening. "Thank you," she whispered. "Remember me not as a witch, but as a healer.
And with that last word, Eleanor's figure faded into light and the room fell silent. That oppressive atmosphere weighing down the mansion was lifted to make way for a feeling of calm and tranquility.
The family, exhausted yet relieved, hugged each other. They had faced the worst of their fears and had come out victorious. The spirit of the witch was finally at rest, and the mansion, once a house of darkness and terror, became a haven of light and peace.
In the days that followed, the Davis family worked to heal from their ordeal. The mansion, now free from its dark past, became a place of healing and renewal. They continued to honor Eleanor's memory, maintaining the shrine in the garden and holding small ceremonies to remember her. The mansion, once seen as a suspect by the community, became a beacon of survival and, finally, hope. Friends and neighbors came by frequently, infusing warmth and joy into the once-haunted house. The Davis family, bonded stronger through their trials, faced this new phase in their lives with gratefulness and resolve.

John and Mary worked on piecing their lives together and gave Lucy and Tom a stable, loving home. The children, still recovering from their ordeal, began to regain their sense of security and happiness. They found solace in the unity of their family and support from their community.

The medium and historian, who had played important parts in their journey, remained close friends and advisors as they helped the family learn the value of acknowledging and accepting the past and looking forward toward a brighter future.

It was now a bright and full-of-love mansion that spoke volumes about the will to survive and the inner strength that lies within the human spirit. The Davis family had faced one of the most fearful and dark times, which had changed them, making them stronger and united like never before.

Finally, the Davis family was not just offered a house; they found a real home-one whose past was regarded and represented, where its future shined bright with all the promises and joys of an end. And so their story became incorporated into the continuance of that mansion, one witness to love and resilience and what understanding and compassion entail.

Chapter 15: Where Hidden Secrets Meet

The Davis family finally seemed to live in a place of serenity, security, and tranquility, after facing so many hellish moments. The mansion became a symbol of their resilience and togetherness. But it didn't last long. One afternoon, while arranging the attic, John found an old, sealed envelope in a dust-filled corner. The envelope, yellow with age, was addressed to Elias Blackwood, who was the original owner of the mansion.

Curiosity aroused, John opened the envelope and found a letter inside. It was in beautiful and neat handwriting, and as he started to read, he noticed it was from a person named Lavinia, who must have been Blackwood's closest confidante. It was a secret ritual that was never completed, the letter said, and there was a hidden chamber beneath the mansion with powerful artifacts and dark magic.

John's heart raced as he read the letter. The mention of a hidden chamber and powerful artifacts was both intriguing and terrifying. He knew he had to share this discovery with Mary and the medium. That evening, he gathered his family in the living room and revealed the contents of the letter.

Mary's eyes widened with concern as she listened. "Another hidden chamber? After everything we've been through, this is the last thing we need," she exclaimed anxiously.

The medium, who by now had really become a friend and an advisor to him, peered closely at the letter. "This ritual Lavinia mentions-it seems to involve calling in and binding powerful entities. If Blackwood left it incomplete, it could explain some of the lingering energy in the house," she explained.

The historian, present in the gathering, gave his views. "Lavinia was known to be Blackwood's most trusted confidante. If she wrote about a hidden chamber, it's likely real. But we must proceed with caution. Uncovering it could unleash forces beyond our control."

While this secretly petrified the family, they all knew and agreed that the hidden chamber had to be found, and whatever was inside needed to be taken care of properly. They couldn't afford another wave of terror like the ones they had faced thus far.

The following morning, the family began to look for this secret room. The letter was very vague as to its location, referencing points of the mansion that no longer existed. The medium suggested using a pendulum to aid in finding the chamber, and after some preparation, they started an earnest search for it.

They looked in every nook and cranny of the mansion, from attic to basement, but found absolutely nothing. As days wore on with no important development, frustration mounted, and tempers flared. The children, sensing their parents' anxiety, tried to do their part, but it was taking its toll.

It was in the evening, when they were just about to call it a day, that Tom, who had been playing in the garden, burst in with an old key he had found buried near the ancient oak. The key was quaintly wrought, with curious symbols stamped upon the metal. The family drew near, their faces lighting up with interest at this unexpected find.

The historian peered closely at the key and found that the symbols on it matched the description in Lavinia's letter. "This must be the key to the hidden chamber," he exclaimed in excitement. "But where does it fit?"

The family decided to focus their efforts in the basement, since it was here that any secret chamber was most likely to be found. They carefully examined every wall and floorboard, searching for even the slightest indication of a hidden entrance. After hours of searching, John noticed, in the far corner of the basement, behind an old bookshelf, a faint outline of what looked like a door.

Whereupon, with renovated resolution, they swept the spot clear and found imbedded in the wall a small keyhole. John inserted the key, and with a soft click, the secret door swung back, revealing a narrow steep staircase leading downward into the very bowels of the mansion.

They crept down the stairs with flashlights, the beam casting an eerie light on the cold stone walls. It got colder with every step downward and became an omen of what would come. Finally, they saw an iron door, large in size, at the bottom of the stairs. This, too, had symbols, very similar to what they found on the key.

With a deep breath, John pushed the door open; a large underground chamber unfolded before his eyes. The room was filled with ancient artifacts, dusty tomes, and bizarre contraptions. Right in the middle of the chamber was an ornate altar circled by dark, twisted statues, which seemed to stare at them with malevolent eyes.

The medium, feeling dark energy in that room, was calling for caution. "Those are powerful, dangerous artifacts-we must be careful not to upset anything," she warned.

As they ventured deeper into the chamber, they found more and more clues that told them about the unfinished ritual Lavinia had mentioned. The altar itself was inscribed with strange symbols and runes, with tomes containing the detailed ways of summoning and binding entities. The family realized this was the heart of Blackwood's dark magic- the source of the supernatural disturbances that had been terrorizing the mansion.

The medium said that some cleansing ritual needed to be performed to nullify the dark energy in the chamber. They gathered the necessary ingredients and began the ritual, chanting ancient incantations and burning sacred herbs. The air grew thick with energy, and the statues seemed to come to life, their eyes glowing with a sinister light.

As the ritual progressed, the ground trembled, and a low, rumbling sound filled the chamber. The family held hands, their voices steady despite the fear that gripped them. The medium's chanting grew louder, and a blinding light filled the room, banishing the darkness and purifying the space. The statues were again inanimate upon the loss of the light, and the oppressive energy was gone. The chamber, once of dark magic, finally converted into a place of peaceful tranquility.

The Davis family, therefore, were overcome with deep relief since the hidden chamber was cleansed and the dark artifacts neutralized. They had faced their biggest fears and finally overcome them, emerging strong and united.

The historian suggested that the chamber be preserved for historical purposes as a witness to the dark past of the mansion and the strength of the family. The medium agreed and said it could serve as a reminder of the power of light over darkness.

John and Mary liked the idea because it would be a way to honor the history of the mansion while making sure future generations understand that their fears should be confronted and overcome. They worked with the historian in detailing their experiences, from the rituals down to the artifacts they had uncovered.

A mansion once viewed suspiciously by the community turned into a hopeful symbol of the people and their strong spirits. The family offers tours and other learning opportunities as a way to share their story and the history behind the mansion. This once-feared mansion is now a place for learning and building inspiration in the community, much like a lighthouse on its shore.

With renewed confidence and a sense of security, Lucy and Tom blossomed in their new environment. They felt proud of their family's history and the steps they took to overcome the dark legacy that had burdened the mansion. They would continue to honor the memory of Eleanor with ceremonies out in the garden, tending the shrine they built.

Grateful and firm, this new life finally greeted the Davies family through united experiences. Their family had faced unimaginable terrors, emerging stronger, more united than ever. And with that, their story became history within the mansion-reminding everybody of love, resilience, and the indomitable strength of the human spirit.

In the end, the Davis family found not just a house but a real home where the past was recognized and respected, and the future was bright with promise and joy. Their story, now a part of the history in the mansion, reminded them that even in the face of darkness, light and love could prevail.

Chapter 16: The Diaries That Haunted

Now, after cleansing the chamber and having rid it of those artifacts that brought upon its darkness, there was renewed peace in this mansion once again. As the family ventured further with restoring the mansion to its old grandeur, a little cabinet stood locked in the library, prompting Mary, ever the detective, to unlock it once again with that very same key found previously inside it, thereby opening up an assemblage of diaries from the previous owner.

All the diaries belonged to the different family members of the Blackwoods, chronicling the long, torrid history of the mansion. Mary hoped that reading them would present more insight into the history of the house and who might have occupied it. She opened the first by Lavinia Blackwood, Elias's confidante.

As Mary read the entries of Lavinia, she was led through a series of unsettling accounts regarding the mansion. She recorded in her diary how Elias had performed all his rituals and experiments that bound Eleanor's spirit. She describes all the strange occurrences and apparitions that plagued the mansion generation after generation.

But one entry in particular caught her eye. Lavinia had written about an unseen presence in the house, a malevolent force that seemed to grow stronger with each passing year. She described how family members would wake up with unexplained bruises, hear disembodied whispers, and feel an oppressive sense of dread.

Now, Mary's heart was racing as she read on and on. Lavinia had surmised that this unseen presence was the spirit of a vengeful ancestor, angered by Elias's dark magic. Lavinia attempted to communicate with the spirit, but her attempts only seemed to anger it further. And then the diary ended abruptly, with an ominous feeling left in the air.

Unable to rid her thoughts of something lurking while in bed that night, Mary kept hearing the incoherent mutterings and door creaking, footsteps out in the corridor, but upon descent, there's nobody. At this point in time, though she knew otherwise deep inside her gut, she made an attempt at reassuring herself this all constituted a figment of her overactive imagination, the unseen presence Lavinia had written her about.

For several nights, the inexplicable events worsened. The kids complained of sleep disturbances and getting unaccountable bruised marks. He heard disembodied whispers calling out his name while Mary felt oppressed anytime she happened to be in a solitary confinement. It hit them that now it was a different sort of entity-more diabolical-which they had never confronted thus far.

With the rise in the intensity of the threat, medium sensed the risen danger and prepared a seer to converse with the spirit, if it arrives. The family sat holding hands with the medium in their living room; the medium resorted to spirits of the light to commence the rite. The air cold, the ambiance grew tense.

The eyes of the medium suddenly rolled and, in a voice not her own, she began to speak. "I am the spirit of Marcus Blackwood, and I demand vengeance for the sins of my descendants. This house is cursed, and all who dwell here shall suffer.".

The family sat in horror as the medium's body began to contort and the furniture in the room started to shake. The medium, now possessed by Marcus's spirit, continued to speak. "Elias's dark magic has bound me here, and I will not rest until I have my revenge.

Desperate to protect his family, John pleaded with the spirit. "We are not responsible for Elias's actions! We just want to live in peace. What can we do to free you?"

It was then that the spirit, speaking through the medium, asked them to find and destroy some powerful artifact, which was hidden in this mansion. Marcus explained that it was a source of his binding and a key to his freedom. When the spirit had left her, she collapsed, exhausted but determined to help the family.

The family began to search for the artifact with increased urgency. They searched every room, basement, and attic, hoping to find anything that resembled Marcus's description. Days turned into weeks, and nothing was found through their search. The malevolent presence in the house grew stronger, and the family's resolve began to break down.

One afternoon of that summer, Lucy was playing in the garden when something felt strange about the big ancient oak tree facing her. It seemed as if the trunk was hollow, and she had never seen that before. Her curiosity got the best of her, and she reached inside and felt something cold and metallic. She pulled out a small, ornate box, covered in strange symbols similar to those they had seen in the hidden chamber.

Lucy ran to show her parents, and the medium immediately recognized the box as the artifact they were searching for. "This is it," she said, her voice filled with both relief and fear. "This is the source of Marcus's binding."

The family gathered around the box, at a loss for what to do. The medium told them that they had to destroy the artifact in some sort of cleansing ritual, similar to the one that they had done in the hidden chamber. She warned them that it would be dangerous, that the spirit would probably try to stop them.

The family prepared for the ritual, determined that this should finally put an end to the haunting. They had all the ingredients ready and prepared an altar in the garden where the ancient oak tree loomed, witness to the dark history of the mansion.

The family now joined around the altar, upon which lay an ornate box at its middle. The medium started the purification ritual, in a low and melodious voice that was somehow vibrating with the earth itself. The air became thick with the surge of energy, and the temperature in the room suddenly plunged.

Then, suddenly, a powerful gust of wind swept across the garden, extinguishing the candles and plunging everything into darkness. The cold, evil presence enveloped the family, who became even colder. The medium's chanting went louder, attempting to ward it off.

Before them stood the ghostly form of Marcus Blackwood, his body dancing in the air like a shadow in the night. "You dare to destroy my binding?" he roared as his voice boomed through the garden. "You shall suffer for this!

The earth shook as Marcus's rage took hold, and the family stood firm, holding hands against the attack. The medium, his voice at a fever pitch, ended his incantation with a flash of light bursting from the altar and bathing the box in its brilliance.

Marcus's form twisted and contorted as the brilliance enveloped him. "No!" he shrieked, his voice an agony of defeat and anger. "You cannot undo what has been done!

With one final, deafening roar, Marcus's form disintegrated, and the light from the altar grew to a blinding crescendo before dying out. The air was still once more, and the crushing feeling of dread that had weighed upon the mansion was lifted. The box lay at the center of the altar, now nothing more than a pile of ash.

The family, exhausted but relieved, embraced each other. They had confronted their darkest fear and won. The malevolent spirit of Marcus Blackwood was finally at peace, and the mansion, once a place of darkness and terror, had become a sanctuary of light and peace.

The Davis family, over the forthcoming weeks, continued to restore the mansion to its former glory but was building a future filled with hope and joy. They shared their story with the community, and the once-feared mansion became a beacon of resilience and strength.

Grateful and resolute, the family that was bonded through all of this got ready to plunge into their new life. The unimaginable horrors faced by them made them emerge as stronger and united than ever. Their story wove itself now into the history of the mansion-a reminder that even in the darkest of times, light and love could prevail.

They finally found something more than a house: a real home where the past was faced and respected, while the future beamed bright with promise and joy. And the story of the Davis family joined in with the history of the mansion, a reminder of the strength of love, resilience, and the indomitable human spirit.

Chapter 17: Return of the Witch

The Davis family had finally harnessed the long, intense ritual that put the spirit of Marcus Blackwood to rest. They believed it marked the end of the mansion's supernatural threats. Renewed vigor was fueled into the restoration of the mansion, along with integrating into their new community. It was not long, however, before this well-earned peace they had gained again began to deteriorate.

One evening, when the family was having a quiet dinner, the temperature in the dining room suddenly dropped. A chilling wind blew through the house, causing the candles to flicker wildly. The family exchanged worried glances, and Mary's heart sank as she realized something was amiss. Then, suddenly, a voice guttural and inhuman shook the dining room. "You have freed Marcus, but your battle is far from over." Sending chills down their spines, Lucy clung onto her mother's hand.

The medium had stayed over with the family to help them get used to their new life, and she definitely recognized the voice. "It's the witch," she whispered, her face pale with dread. "She's back."

The family had learned from the diaries that the witch was a powerful sorceress who was hanged many years ago for her dark practices. According to Lavinia's diary, the witch had placed a curse on the Blackwood family and promised to return to inflict evil upon anyone who dared to set their foot in the mansion.

It soon dawned on the family that the defeat of Marcus freed the witch's spirit. The feeling in the air became thick with the presence of something very malevolent, and the Davis family knew they had to move fast if they were to contain this new threat before it consumed them.

The witch did not waste any time, and on that night, while Mary lay in bed, she heard from afar a voice with a particular evil whisper. She opened her eyes to see a figure standing at the foot of her bed, its eyes shining with an eerie green light. Mary tried to scream, but immediately her voice caught in her throat.

The bony hand reached out and touched her arm-a cold, burning sensation. And in an instant, it was gone, leaving behind a dark bruise upon her skin. Mary hastily rushed to awaken John and the children and warned them of the witch's presence.

The medium confirmed their suspicion. "The witch is trying to scare us, to weaken our resolve. We cannot let her succeed," she said. She recommended having a protection ritual to defend the family against the witch's malevolent attack.

First, everyone had to gather in the living room, lighting candles and burning sage to purify him. The medium asked them to perform a chant for protection by spirits of light. While the chanting was taking place, it became hotter and hotter outside, but finally, the heavy vibe in the house started releasing itself. They all knew this would be temporary relief.

The next morning, the family in the mansion saw strange symbols of ash on the walls. The historian, who was helping them decipher some of the house's history, recognized the symbols to be ancient runes, the ones used in dark magic. "The witch tries to claim her territory," he explained. "We need to find a way to remove these symbols and weaken her power."

Determined to protect their home, the family set to work scrubbing the symbols off the walls and performing cleansing rituals. However, the witch's attacks grew more frequent and intense: disembodied screams in the night, objects flying across rooms, ghostly apparitions of the witch hanging from the ancient oak tree in the garden.

With a newfound sense of hope, the family turned back to the diaries they had found in the library. Mary found a hidden diary, previously unknown and secreted away behind a loose floorboard, belonging to the witch herself. The pages contained an intimate account of her life, dark practices, and the curse she had placed on the Blackwood family.

The diary revealed that this witch, known as Morgana, had been a great sorceress feared and worshipped in equal measure in her lifetime. She lived in the mansion long before the Blackwood family ever did, performing many dark rituals in its concealed chambers. After the townspeople found out about her practices, they captured and hanged her, but she had time to curse the mansion and all those who would inhabit it in the future.

Morgana's diary explained in detail the powerful spells and rituals she had cast to bind her spirit to the mansion. She had fashioned several talismans and placed them around, anchoring her spirit to this world. These were the keys that would free the mansion from her evil presence.

These talismans needed to be found and destroyed, but the diary only provided very cryptic clues as to where they could be. They decided to start their search in the garden, where they had seen the apparition of the witch.

Buried amidst its roots, while digging around that old oak tree, they came upon a small exquisitely carved box; inside, it pulsed with an unusual crystal radiating light. The medium identified it as one of the witch's talismans. A cleansing ritual was done in order to nullify its power, hence rendering it destroyed.

With the first talisman destroyed, it would appear that the witch's presence weakened. The air was lighter in the mansion, and the oppressive energy was lesser. Yet, they knew they had more work to do.

Continuing, using the clues of Morgana's diary, they still had to find the other talismans: in the fireplace, up in the attic, and beneath the ground of their basement. With every destroyed talisman, the presence of the witch got weaker, yet every next attack she was getting more desperate and brutal.

One night, while they were about to destroy the last talisman, the witch appeared before them in a more solid and terrifying form than ever. "You think you can banish me?" she snarled, her voice echoing through the mansion. "I will never leave this place. You will all suffer!"

The witch attacked with a ferocity that shook the walls and sent things flying around the room. The family held hands, undaunted. The medium started an incantation of invocation to the spirits of light to come and assist them.

The air was electric with energy as the witch and medium clashed in a frenzied battle of wills. The family joined in the chant, their voices steady despite the chaos erupting around them. The witch's form flickered and wavered, her power waning as the final talisman was destroyed.

With one final, deafening scream, the witch form disintegrated, and the oppressive energy released in the mansion. The air grew still, and the house was imbued with a new sense of peacefulness. Exhausted, yet triumphant, the family embraced each other. They had faced their biggest fear and were victorious.

With each passing week, the Davis family did not stop in reorganizing the mansion. They put everything back to normal, preserving its history for a bright and joyful future. They shared their story with the community, as this once-feared mansion became a symbol of resilience and strength.

United in experience, the family grasped their new life with gratitude and determination. The unimaginable horrors they had passed through seemed to have left them more solid than before, joined as one whole, united. Now their story mingled with the history of the mansion: when there was darkness, light and love could prevail.

In the end, the Davis family found not only a house but also a home—a place where their past was preserved and respected, and where their future was bright and filled with hope. Their story, too, became a part of the mansion's history, one of love, strength, and the unyielding resolve of the human spirit.

Chapter 18: The Last Stand

With the destruction of the last talisman, it would appear that peace finally came to the mansion. Still, the Davis family kept guard. The presence of the witch could still be felt, and they knew this was not yet over. A final confrontation, they felt, was lurking, and one needed to prepare for that battle.

The medium, having stayed with the family through thick and thin of their struggles, gathered them in the living room. "Morgana's spirit is weakened but not yet banished," she explained. "We must perform one last, powerful ritual to cleanse the mansion completely. This will be our final stand against her."

Over the next few days, the family collected the herbs, candles, and other sacred objects instructed by the medium to use in the ritual. John was determined to protect his family, and he reinforced the entrances to the mansion, preparing everyone for the coming battle.

Mary and the children sanctified one area of the great hall within the mansion, the central heart of the house. Anointing the floor and walls with symbols of protection, they created a circle of safety within which to perform the ritual. The historian, by now a close friend, was supportive in researching some of the most ancient rites that might help them in their struggle.

The feeling of the witch's presence became a little more pronounced with time as they all worked. They felt the eyes unseen watching them pass, the impression of dread always hanging over them in the air. Afraid, yet showing great acts of bravery, determination beyond that seen in one their age, after being thrown into every imaginable horror in life.

On the night of the ritual, with hearts beating and filled with a mix of fear and determination, the family came together in the great hall. At the very heart of the circle stood the medium, leading the family into an invocation chant in the name of the spirits of light and protection. As the ritual began, the air grew thick with energy: the voices rang in sweet harmony.

With every chant, the room grew colder and a sinister wind whirled through the hall. The candles flickered and dimmed, casting eerie shadows on the walls. And then, in an instant, the witch's form materialized before them, her eyes burning with malevolent fire. "You cannot banish me!" she hissed, her voice echoing through the hall. "This house is mine!"

The family continued to chant, undaunted by the menacing presence of Morgana. The medium raised her hands, directing the energy of the ritual at the witch. Radiant light shone from the protective symbols on the walls, creating a barrier holding the witch at bay.

Morgana's form flickered and wavered as the energy of the ritual built up. In a shriek of anger, she hurled a barrage of dark energy against the family. Objects flew across the room, and the walls shook with the force of her attack. But the protective barrier held strong, and the family's resolve remained unbroken.

Seizing her chance, Mary stepped forward and addressed the witch. "You have plagued this house and the people in it for far too long," she said, standing her ground. "Your time here is at an end. We won't let you harm us anymore." The witch's eyes narrowed now, and she unleashed her fury upon Mary. But the chant of the family grew louder, their voices together in one mighty crescendo. The medium, taking in all the energy from the ritual, put all her strength into calling out the spirit of the witch.

Now that the ritual was at its height, Morgana's attacks were growing ever more desperate. The walls shook and crackled with dark energy as the twisted, contorted form of the witch flailed about, her rage evident in every jerky movement. The family stood united, hands clasped together with combined strength against the malevolent spirit.

At this, a determined John stepped forward, advancing to stand alongside Mary. "This is our home," he said resolutely. "We are going to defend it and our family against everything.

The witch's form flickered as she threw a powerful blast of dark energy toward John and Mary. The barrier protecting them wavered, but the chant of the family held firm. The medium, her voice high above the tumult, called out to the spirits of light for their assistance in battle.

With the energy reaching a fever pitch in the room, the form of the witch started to break down. "No!" she wailed. Anguish and anger sounded forth from her screams: "You shall never conquer me!"

But their family was resolute. Renewed chanting in unison made their voices lift up into a melodious hymn that was somehow knitted into the very essence of the house. The protecting symbols on the walls blazed brighter, their light forcing back the darkness.

With one last, deafening roar, the witch's form shattered, and a blinding light filled the room. The oppressive energy lifted, and the air grew still. The family dropped to the floor, exhausted but triumphant, their bodies shaking with relief.

The medium, her face carved with exhaustion, smiled weakly. "It's over," she said, her voice barely above a whisper. "Morgana's spirit has been banished. The house is finally free."

As the following days went by, an atmosphere of peace and ease developed within this mansion. There would be no more darkness-a heaviness on their dwelling site-and with hope and light, there developed tranquility in every heart. The Davis continued through restoration on every edge, retaining bits and scraps with historical meaning but bringing life inside at all dimensions where hopes and brightness touch hearts, their spirits.

This gallantry from the family inspired the community to rally around them. What was once a mansion of horror and a place to be avoided now became a beacon of resilience and strength. The story of the Davis family spread like wildfire through town-a story of love and determination against unimaginable horrors.

Closer than ever before, John and Mary worked untiringly to restore the mansion to its old glory. They incorporated protective symbols into the decoration of the mansion, reminding them of their victory over the darkness. The children also accepted their new life with gratitude and joy; their bravery and resilience were reflected in everything they did.

The historian became a close friend and helped them document their experiences. Together, they recorded all the history that had taken place in the mansion: the battles, the ones they had won. This was a record of how strong they were and just how light can always be at the end of the tunnel.

With her task at an end, the medium got ready to leave the mansion. She embraced each member of the family, her eyes brimming with pride and gratitude. "You have faced great darkness and emerged victorious," she said. "Your strength and love have brought light to this house. Remember that, always."

The family watched the medium leave, feeling words of gratitude beyond words for guidance and support. They realized that as much as their journey had encompassed danger and fear, it had brought them closer together, stronger. In the end, the Davis family found not just a house but a true home where the past was acknowledged and respected, and the future was filled with promise and joy. Their story became a part of the mansion's legacy and a testament to the power of love, resilience, and the enduring strength of the human spirit.

Standing together in the garden as the sun rose to a new day, the Davis family was filled with hope and gratitude. They had confronted their deepest fears and overcome them, held fast by their love and resolve. And in the freshness of this new dawn, they knew that nothing would ever shake their unbreakable bond or their indomitable spirit.

Chapter 19: A Haunted History

With the immediate threat of the witch's spirit gone, the Davis family felt a sense of relief and newfound peace. But there was still so much to be learned about the mansion, and they were determined to find out everything there was to know about its haunted history. They felt that the only way to ensure a bright future for their home was to understand its past.

The historian, by now an invaluable ally, suggested a deep study of the history of the mansion. "We need to know all the details, all the stories this house has to tell," he said. "Only then can we understand the forces that have molded it."

Mary and John agreed, and thus the investigation became serious and regular. The diaries and journals that had been found gave way to an intense scrutiny once again in search of any more hidden details about the gloomy past of the mansion. Children rummaged through each house in order to find secret rooms and any other documents.

One day, when Lucy and Tommy were rummaging through the attic, they found an old trunk tucked away in one corner. Opening it, they found letters, photographs, and personal effects belonging to the Blackwood family. The letters told about the history of the family-their triumphs and tragedies.

As they read through the letters, a story sent them chills. It told of Eliza Blackwood, a young woman who had lived in the mansion during the late 1800s. She was a gifted medium, able to speak with spirits. Trying to warn her family about the dark forces lurking in the house, her warnings fell on deaf ears.

The letters said that Eliza was holding seances to understand and keep at bay such evil spirits. She had caught the attention of Morgana, the witch, who wanted to use Eliza's powers for her own evil reasons. Her last letters spoke about the terrible fight with Morgana and how she had sacrificed herself so that Morgana would not take her anger out on her family.

Discovering the story of Eliza added other textures to the depth of the history of the mansion. The family really took to Eliza, finding an affinity with her in the midst of darkness; to be sure, they had battled their own wars. They kept a room for her memory and filled it with her letters and many old photographs, her personal belongings scattered across her bed.

The family felt grateful as they moved further in every nook and corner, determined to leave nothing hidden. They concentrated on those parts of the house that they had left unexplored, hoping that more clues would reveal much about the haunted history of the mansion.

One afternoon, while searching the basement, he discovered a door hidden behind some old crates; it was iron-reinforced and had all the appearances of not having been opened in decades. The door was opened with trepidation, the family gathering around to see what secrets were beyond.

Behind the door, they found a narrow corridor opening into a row of small rooms, each connected by internal doors. The air was heavy with dust, and the walls were lined with shelves that were filled with books, artifacts, and other strange, ancient objects. He identified the rooms as a secret library and occult research facility, likely utilized by Morgana and subsequent residents in studying and practicing dark magic.

Carefully examining the contents of the rooms, they found a collection of grimoires and spellbooks, some of which were written in languages they couldn't understand. The medium, who had returned to assist with their investigation, recognized many of the symbols and incantations as powerful and dangerous.

Among them was a book that turned out to be the diary belonging to one Edmund Blackwood, a long-ago relative of Marcus. Edmund had been a scholar of the occult, and in his diary were detailed experiments with summoning and binding spirits. He had become obsessed with the idea of controlling the malevolent entities haunting the mansion, believing he could harness their energy for his purposes.

Edmund's diary led them to a secret ritual chamber where he conducted the most hazardous experiments. The chamber was at the far end of the corridor, its walls covered in various carvings and symbols. They could feel a thick atmosphere of doom, like some sort of presence, as they entered.

The medium warned them that the chamber was still charged with dark energy and great caution should be taken. She showed ways of performing a cleansing ritual to neutralize any lingering malevolence, showing at the same time respect due unto the spirits trapped here.

As they completed the ritual, the air inside the chamber started to get warmer and the heavy atmosphere started to clear. It was as if the spirits that were bound here finally gained release. They sealed the chamber and promised themselves never to use it again for dark purposes.

In their continued exploration of the mansion, the family found one room that had been sealed for many years. The room was on the third floor, dust-covered, with old, faded portraits hanging from the walls. Among those portraits, one really stood out: a big, imposing painting of a woman with piercing eyes and a stern expression. A plaque beneath the portrait identified her as Lavinia Blackwood, the matriarch of the Blackwood family.

As soon as she saw the portrait, the medium had immediately sensed a powerful presence. "There is more to this portrait than meets the eye," she said, "It contains a piece of Lavinia's spirit and that energy is very alive, very potent."

The family shivered as they looked upon the portrait. Wherever they walked in that room, it seemed as if Lavinia's eyes were following, her frowning upon them. The medium explained that Lavinia was an extremely powerful witch and how her spirit had been attached to the portrait, overseeing the mansion.

That night, strange happenings started to occur around the house. The family heard footsteps echo through the halls, doors creaking open and shut of their own accord, and Lavinia's portrait seemed to glow with an eerie light. Lucy and Tommy reported seeing a ghostly figure of Lavinia roaming the halls, her eyes filled with anger and sorrow.

The medium surmised that Lavinia's spirit was troubled because the mansion had been disturbed by the recent events. She offered to hold a seance to communicate with Lavinia and understand her grievances. The family agreed, hoping to find a way to put Lavinia's spirit to rest.

During the seance, the medium called upon Lavinia's spirit, asking her to reveal her presence. The air grew cold and the candles flickered as a ghostly figure materialized before them. Lavinia's spirit appeared, her eyes filled with a mixture of rage and sadness. "Why have you disturbed my home?" she demanded, her voice echoing through the room.

Mary spoke for the family, explaining their situation and how they would love to know more about the history of the mansion. She assured her that they didn't mean any harm and wanted to honor the Blackwood family's legacy. Lavinia's expression softened, and she began to recount her story.

Lavinia explained to him that she was the keeper of the mansion and that it had been entrusted to her for protection against dark forces. She had been fighting Morgana and other evil spirits, using all her powers for the protection of the mansion. But since she died, her spirit had stuck to the portrait, trapping her and not being able to protect the house as before.

The family listened with compassion, understanding the burden Lavinia had carried. They promised to honor her legacy and protect the mansion from any further threats. The medium performed a ritual to release Lavinia's spirit from the portrait and let her finally rest in peace.

With Lavinia's spirit at peace, the mansion seemed lighter and friendlier. The family continued their restorations, infusing the mansion with its own history. They even made a memorial room for Lavinia and Eliza and the other spirits that watched over the house, filling it with portraits and letters and artifacts of remembrance.

The community was so inspired by the family's commitment and bravery that it also embraced the mansion as a symbol of resilience and a link to history. The historian helped the family organize tours and events that showcased the rich history of the mansion, along with stories of former occupants. The mansion became a place of learning and contemplation where one could pay their respects to the struggles and triumphs of those who had come first.

United in experience, the completeness found a new meaning within the house for the Davis family. They had gone through unimaginable horrors and emerged stronger, their bond unbreakable. Their story joined the legacy of the mansion-testimony to love, resilience, and strength eternal of the human spirit.

As the sun set on another day, the Davis family gathered in the garden, their hearts filled with hope and gratitude. They had uncovered the haunted history of their home and brought peace to the spirits that once tormented them. In the light of the setting sun, they knew they could face any challenge that came their way, secure in the knowledge that their bond was unbreakable and their spirit indomitable.

Chapter 20: New Beginnings

The haunted history of the mansion was by now well explored and finally laid to rest; thus, a healing process began for the Davis family. Gone was the oppressive energy that once plagued their home, replaced instead by tranquility and hope. They could actually begin making new memories and establishing a sense of normalcy.

Projects abound, and together, the family worked at breathing life back into the mansion. John and Mary planted flowers and cut back trees, restoring a most beautiful garden left to wither away, thereby creating an especial haven in which they were most happy to just be as family. The garden was a sign of their new life, a place where they could sit and contemplate how far they'd come, enjoy the peace that they struggled so hard for.

Inside the house, children helped to renew rooms-making them warm and full of character. They chose bright colors, comfortable furniture, and decorations associated with their different interests. No more was the house dark and foreboding; it was filled with laughter and light.

The community, who had been supportive during the Davis family's ordeal, continued to help and befriend them. Neighbors would often visit with gifts in hand, sharing stories and news. What was once feared and avoided now became a house of refuge, where the community came together as one, in resilience and unity.

By now, the historian had become a family friend and helped them trace their experiences, along with the history of the mansion. They made sure that a detailed account of the events that transpired would be left behind so that future generations would know the importance of the mansion and the bravery of those who had lived there.

The Davis family was willing to mark this as a point of culmination from their journey, celebrating the dawn of a new era. They invited their friends, neighbors, and everybody who had helped them through all that they endured. The party wasn't actually one but an act of praise and recognition regarding the history of the mansion and the spirits which once habitated it.

The garden now was in full bloom, and the event was held within its midst. Tables were set up with delicious food, and the sound of music and laughter wafted through the air. The family gave tours of the mansion and shared stories of their experiences and the history they had unraveled. The memorial room, dedicated to Lavinia and Eliza and other spirits, drew admiration and respect from all who came to visit.

The medium gave a final blessing at the celebration to keep the mansion a place of peace and light. She spoke about remembering the past but also embracing the future-a feeling that deeply touched all present.

John and Mary took a moment to address their guests,

conveying their appreciation for all the support and love they had received. "The journey has been so difficult," John added with a high pitch of emotion. "At the same time, it has shown us the family's strength and the power of our community. We are grateful to all of you for standing by our side."

Mary added, "We have learned so much about the history of this mansion and the people who lived here before us. We will continue to honor their memory and see that the home remains a place of love and light."

The night was well spent rejoicing, with laughter and an aftertaste of achievement. It had brought a family closer to a sense of closure, knowing they had faced their biggest fears and come out stronger. Where the mansion had once represented darkness, it was now a beacon of hope and resilience.

As the days went into weeks and then to months, life settled down. This mansion, with such great history, finally grew to become what every home must wish: newfound peacefulness amidst love and warmth. And into that love continued the Davis family through the processes of restoration and remembrance to be continued from generation to future generation in this mansion.

With his further assistance, they were able to compile an impressive archive concerning the history of the mansion, with letters, photos, and items they found in the place. This became accessible to all outsiders, as this attracted several historians, researchers, and simply interested visitors wanting to learn something more about this story-like mansion.

It also established the Eliza and Lavinia Foundation in memory, to underwrite local history projects and the preservation of historic homes-a testimony to the commitment they felt toward honoring the past while building a better future.

One evening, when the family gathered in the garden, they took a drive down memory lane. "We've been through so much," John said as he looked at his family. "But we come out stronger on the other side. This mansion taught us a lesson on the important features of resilience and the power of love.

Mary nodded, a small smile on her face. "We've faced our fears and overcome them. And in doing so, we've created a home filled with joy and hope."

The children had things to say now: confident, resilient. "I'm proud of what we've done here," Lucy said. "We have taken a place of fear and turned it into a home of love."

Tommy added, "And we have made so many new friends in the process. This mansion is something more than just being a house; it is part of the family."

The family sat together in the garden, feeling quite contented as the sun set, casting a warm glow over the flowers and trees. They knew that their journey was far from over, but they were ready to face whatever the future held. This mansion, its rich history, and enduring legacy would always be a testament to their strength and love.

Having enshrined the past and taken hope from the present, the Davis family was thus excitedly and anxiously looking into the future. They had turned a mansion into a home with love and warmth; now, whatever came next was met with acceptance.

They both continued to work on different projects within and outside the mansion. They put up a community garden and invited neighbors to work with them in planting and harvesting. The garden became a connection and collaboration spot, binding people together within the community.

With the inspiration of these experiences, the children went after their interests with renewed vigor. Lucy had taken an avid interest in history, helping along with research and documentation with the historian often. Tommy studied folklore and mythology since he was fascinated by anything beyond the realm of reality.

It was now a symbol of resilience and hope, attracting visitors from all corners of the globe. They came to learn about its history, to see the memorial room, and to experience the peace that now permeated its walls. The Davis family opened their arms to such visitors, sharing their story and what they had learned in the process.

The family remained steadfast as they forged ahead in preserving the legacy of the mansion and simultaneously creating a bright future. They realized that though the journey so far had brought changes in their lives, it had created an indelible mark in the community and elsewhere.

One evening, the family sat around a bonfire in the garden, reflecting on how far they had come. "We've come so far," John said, his voice full of pride. "And we've created something truly special here."

Mary nodded, her eyes shining with happiness. "This mansion will always be a part of us. It's a testament to our strength and our love."

The other children, seated nearby, nodded and smiled in agreement. "We've faced our fears and come out stronger," Lucy said. "And we've made a home that we can be proud of."

Tommy added, "This mansion is filled with history, but it's also filled with our memories. It's a place where we can grow and thrive."

The Davis family sat before the crackling fire under the

bright star-filled sky in complete peace and satisfaction. They had experienced the most unimaginable horrors but came out on top, and it was a bond not to be shaken. They realized that the coming years would host many challenges; however, this they would also face together.

The fire in the night was their light; the beauty of the garden surrounded them, and the warmth of their family kept them so. The Davis family was optimistic, looking with excitement toward what was yet to come. They had built a home filled with love and light where the past was revered, yet the future shone bright. And at the core of their dear house, they were certain they would overcome anything thrown at them because they knew well that nothing was as strong as the ties binding them and a spirit unconquerable.

www.ingramcontent.com/pod-product-compliance
Lightning Source LLC
LaVergne TN
LVHW012023060526
838201LV00061B/4434